I0572155

A Tangle of Yarns

Anthology

of short pieces

by

Members of the Writing Creatively

Groups

at

Kalamunda Community Learning Centre

ISBN: 978-0-6455254-7-2

A catalogue record for this book is available from the National Library of Australia

Published by Tania Park Publishing.

Cover Design: Karen Roberts – Mortimer and White

A Tangle of Yarns

Introduction

This anthology of prose and poetry has been created by the Writing Creatively, Monday and Tuesday morning classes of the Kalamunda Community Learning Centre.

It is with great thanks, pleasure and pride that Tania and I, the class tutors, acknowledge the members of our marvellous team of: Alwena, Cynthia, Dianne, Dot, Graham, Janelle, Janusz, Nicole, Sue, Theo and Victoria, who have created for us the characters and stories of this anthology.

We trust you find reflected in their work the sense of friendship, dedication and talent which has been a joy for us both. Each has contributed several pieces to the anthology, in the form of either prose or poetry. With special thanks to those who assisted in the editing process, and to Karen Roberts who beautifully illustrated the front cover.

Tania Park
Garry Davies

Contents

Curtain Call
Su Watson

Carla looked up from her ironing. The shadows that filled the room made it difficult to see if she was winning her battle against the wrinkles or not. Damn, she'd hoped to get all the work shirts done before she stopped, but here it was almost teatime and there were still two to go. Well, they'd need to wait because Gemma would be yelling for her tea any minute now, and Devon would get home from work soon, starving as usual.

She set the iron back in its rack and hurried to draw the curtains. The fine day that had seen her dry all her laundry outdoors had turned into a fine evening. She paused, her hand on the heavy drapes, to look at the luminous silver of the darkening sky. The colour was odd. The hue more associated with jewellery, like the pendant she wore, than an evening sky. She glanced down at her necklace and smiled. Her father had made it for her in the little shed at the bottom of his garden. He often complained about the pungent smell, but he always came back to working with silver and had produced many beautiful pieces over the years. She wondered what he was doing at this moment. Was he thinking of her, too?

As Carla returned to the curtains, her eye caught movement outside. In the shadows at the bottom of the garden, a large bird landed on the fence. A night for oddities. By now, most of the garden birds were long gone. Tucked up in… wherever garden birds went at nighttime. In any case, it was unusual to see a bird of this size in a garden, here in suburbia. She leaned forward and put her face to the window, cupping her hands round her eyes to get a better view. An owl maybe? She peered into the gloom, her breath fogging the glass. She stood back to wipe it with her sleeve, but when she looked again, the bird had gone. Had she imagined it— mistaken the shape of the fence post amongst the trees for something else? She shook herself and laughed. finally shutting out the night and encasing the room in the warm, pink reflection of the heavy curtains.

Upstairs, she heard Gemma happily chatting to herself as she played.

'Time for tea, Kiddo,' she called up the stairs, before entering the kitchen to dish up a small portion of casserole from the slow cooker so it could cool. When Carla returned to the bottom of the stairs, she could still hear her daughter giggling and chatting, not yet making the move to come down for her tea.

'Gemma, did you hear me?' Carla called. 'Wash your hands now and come down for tea.' She stood and waited till her daughter reluctantly appeared at the top of the staircase. 'Did you wa…'

'Man in my room, Mummy!'

Carla mounted the stairs, taking two at a time before she could even process what Gemma had said. The tight ball of fear in her stomach propelled her to the top step, where she reached for her daughter and drew her into her arms.

'What man?'

Gemma wriggled in her mother's too tight embrace.

'What man?' repeated her mother.

Gemma shrugged; her two-year-old language not advanced enough to articulate further. 'Ow! Hurt me!' she complained.

'Who hurt you? The man? Did the man hurt you?' Carla released Gemma and flew into her daughter's room, her teeth bared, and her fists clenched, ready for battle. Carla stopped in the centre of the room. There was a faint smell—gas… no… garlic… no. Something else, but the thought slipped away as she replayed her daughter's words. Carla did a swift 360°, peering under the bed and into the cupboard as she went. There at the end of the bed was Gemma's small table, set carefully for two with her tea-set, but of the man there was no sign. Carla stalked into each of the upstairs rooms in turn. Checking the windows and the cupboards and under the beds.

When she returned, her daughter was quietly putting her toys away in her big blue box. Carla again noticed that the small table set for two and a glimmer of understanding penetrated her confusion.

'Were you having a tea party, Sweet Pea?'

Gemma nodded.

'With your dolls?'

Gemma shook her head.

'Who then?'

'Man,' answered Gemma. 'Not hurt me. Nice man. Kind man. Gone now,' she said sadly.

Carla felt her shoulders relax. She took a deep breath. Just make believe.

'Sorry if I held you too tight, Sweet Pea. I didn't mean to hurt you.'

Gemma nodded and took Carla's hand.

'I hungry,' she said.

As Carla turned off the bedroom light, she glanced back into Gemma's room. The hair on her arms rippled. She caught her breath. Two shining eyes peered back at her through the bedroom window. The bird blinked slowly and cocked its head to one side. Momentarily distracted by the key in the lock downstairs, she turned to her daughter, who was already releasing her hand.

'Daddeee.'

When Carla looked back, she saw only her tired face reflected in the window. She crossed the room and closed the bedroom curtains.

Carla could hear the TV as she descended to the ground floor and frowned. Devon knew better than to put Gemma in front of the goggle box when it was teatime. What was he thinking? She was about to ask him, but his expression when he came out of the TV room made her pause.

'What is it, Love? Had a bad day?'

He took her hand and led her into the kitchen.

'I had a call as I left work,' he said hesitantly.

She waited, but he said nothing as he struggled to find the words. She looked down at the little charm swinging at the end of her necklace. Percipience stabbed at her heart as two amber eyes stared unblinkingly back from the little owl pendant. Her heart clenched.

'My dad's dead, isn't he?'

'I'm sorry,' he said. 'Did your mum call already? I thought she wanted me to be here… to be with...'

Carla ran to the window and threw back the curtains. As Devon switched on the patio light, a large owl launched itself into the night sky. She desperately tried to catch a final glimpse of the bird through the glass.

'Goodbye, Dad,' she whispered.

Footprints in The Dust
Dianne Morton

The man and his dog have departed, leaving the desert land they once roamed together. Only their footprints remain and soon they too, will disappear with the coming of the rainy season.

A small boy wanders alone, unable to follow the footprints of the only family he has known. Before the changing of the seasons, he searches for the footprints in the dust, but his family will never return. The aunties have no choice but to take him into their community. The child's mother, who was once part of their family, and the father, believed to be a prospector, cannot be found. The boy is not one of them, but he is not of the white folk either.

He grows up protected within the desert community, the streets are his playground. He learns to swim in the waterholes, ride bikes on streets that have no cars, and play footy on the dust-bowl oval. He was often seen kicking a football after school with the other kids in the hot dry paddocks. The football had seen better days, its leather cracked and worn, the stitching barely holding it together. The little feet kicking it have no shoes, but they have never worn shoes, and prefer the freedom of bare feet. They are happy, the small boy and his mates. They dream of one day becoming great footballers, like the teams they saw on the TV at the local.

When a city football team visited the community, the young boy was as excited as all the other boys, as it was a rare treat. They laughed and played football with their heroes under the hot outback sun and for a while they were equals to the city kids.

At the end of the day, he found something that he claimed as his, even though he knew it should be returned to the team who left it behind on the dust-bowl oval. Hiding it under his thread-bare shirt, he ran back to the house he called home and hid his treasure underneath the floorboards, amongst the cobwebs. Not a soul knew he had it and it remained hidden, he didn't want to share it.

At the age of twelve, the community decided the young boy would leave them to study in the city, far away to the south. They gave him the white name Deon. He had excelled in his grades at the local school and given the opportunity, would be able to find his place in the outside world. He took with him, one treasured possession and little else.

Deon hated the city; he didn't understand the rules of living in the boarding school and longed to run free with his mates from the desert. He was often punished for some misdemeanour, as he tried to live in a world he didn't belong in. He stayed though, made a few mates and by the age of sixteen had finished high school with good grades.

The boarding school could no longer offer him a place to continue his studies, and with no scholarship available to cover the costs of his education, it was time to leave. The community belonged in his past and would offer him no further support. The school council found him a job as an apprentice mechanic at the local garage and accommodation at a run-down bed and breakfast. There was never any mention of him returning to the local community. His football dream was what kept him in the city. He played in the local team, and he played well, but he didn't have the backing to make it all the way. His dream of playing football was not to be, even though he had been the best footballer in his school.

As Deon continued working, he longed for the freedom and open spaces of the desert. He ran with a different crowd now. They fixed the cars, then raced them along the streets, or they took cars that were not theirs to take. Joyriding into the early hours of the morning, managing to avoid the law, but only just. It was what they did together. His dream of being someone was no longer a reality. He lived life on the edge, always wondering if he had a future, or would he be another forgotten statistic. He didn't belong in the desert community, and he didn't belong here in the city.

They saw it first, his mates, a revved-up sports car, driving up and down the streets of their neighbourhood. He had come to hang with them after a long day at work and they told him about the sports car. They were all excited and planned to find this car and take it for a joy ride. For it would race faster than any of the cars they had driven so far. It didn't matter that it was not theirs to take.

Deon was not sure, for the law had nearly caught them on the last joy ride, but they were his mates and he needed them. They found the car easily enough late that night. Jobe soon had it running and then they headed out of town, following the roads that wound their way along the coast. As they left the city lights behind, Jobe put his foot hard to the floor and they felt the roar of the powerful engine. Jobe couldn't hold it though, on the bends of the road, as he wasn't an experienced driver. Deon seated in the back, watched in horror as the car became airborne, crashed through the safety barriers. He heard the screams of the others, the roar of the waves below, then silence.

He woke to voices calling out, stunned but alive. It took until daylight before they got him to the top of the cliff face. Deon wanted to ask about his mates, but no words came. He drifted off, to voices telling him how lucky he was to survive.

Deon dreamed then, of a man and his dog who had departed, never to return, leaving behind nothing but footprints in the dust and a small boy. Of running with his mates, kicking a worn-out football, while his treasure lay hidden under the house. He remembered the aunts who took a small boy in, then sent him far away because he wasn't one of them. He wondered if they would remember him or would the memory of him be washed away like the coming of the wet, just like the footprints in the dust.

He escaped the crash with a few broken bones, his mates weren't so lucky. Recovery took time. He sat on the sidelines, watched his football team, and realized his life was going nowhere. He needed to find a way forward, or he would become another person lost and alone. However to find his future, he first needed to face the past.

The community was as he remembered, the same worn-out houses, the dusty streets, and the dust-bowl oval. Deon needed to know about the man and his dog and how it fitted into his young life, as it was only a faded memory. The aunts shook their heads when asked, for they only knew that the stranger wasn't Deon's father but had taken him in after his mother fled the community.

This wasn't his life anymore, there was nothing left here for him to find. He would never know who his father was. Deon watched the little kids playing football, then he left the community forever. He replaced the one thing that he had taken from the community years ago with a brand-new football for the kids to play with.

Back in the city, in the shabby flat he called home, he stopped to think, remembered the two mates taken too early in life, which also could have been his fate. He thought of the past, the man and his dog, his parents that he would never know and the aunts who sent him away. He had a choice to make, continue the way he was living, hating the world and his life or he could change, find a better way to live. It was his to choose, and it had to start now, before it became too late.

You
Theo Pabst

Regardless of the consequences, you do what you want to do all the time and then leave the people around you to pick up the pieces in your wake. You do not take any responsibility for your actions, do you? You must be the slowest learner ever known, or are you just naturally dumb? It is about time you grew up and took responsibility for your actions, if you have any.

John and Tom stood face-to-face - the tension palpable. This scene had played out countless times, a cycle of conflict that seemed to have no end. The absence of hope had become a void that seemed to grow with each repetition.

'You have lived in this house for the last six years, and you still have not adjusted to the style of life required in this household. It was well known that most males are stubborn, but your stubbornness takes the cake. You have stretched your welcome to the point where your place in this household has become untenable. It requires further resolution for you to remain.'

The harsh words thrown at you seemed to have little effect, and without a trace of regret or protest, you turned and gracefully leapt off the sideboard. As you made your way to the kitchen, where your meal awaited, you left yours-truly to clean up the mess you left behind.

It was never a favourite vase, so its loss was not a great tragedy. How could you be blamed for its demise? Thank you, Tom, for your understanding.

Boy
Tania Park
First place – 2023 – Armadale Literary Competition

Boy pricked his ears at the faint hum. The hum turned into a rumble. He lifted his head, eyes alert, but sighed and dropped his chin back onto his paws. It wasn't the right noise. Even the bang of a car door wasn't right. There was no high-pitched squeak designed to hurt his ears.

Scrapes approached the steps outside – three thumps up, two thuds across the boards and loud bangs on the door.

'Coming.'

Boy rolled his eyes towards the big one and they followed her as she hurried down the passage to open the door. Since the new voice wasn't familiar, Boy ignored the yabbering, closed his eyes to wait. It had been longer than usual. Never before had he had to wait so long. He'd been ordered to stay so he stayed. The new voice ceased. The door closed and footsteps neared. At the pause he lifted his tail, gave it a thump and sighed.

'You okay, Boy?' A soft hand ran down his back but it wasn't the right hand. This one didn't edge under the collar to scritch and massage. This one wasn't big and rough. Long splayed fingers didn't run down his spine to ease away the ache.

'You haven't eaten.' The pellets rattled as his bowl was shoved close to his nose. He sniffed, opened his eyes, glanced up, shifted his snout away and closed his eyes with a sigh.

'You must eat, Boy. Grandpa would want you to eat.'

At the word Grandpa, he twitched his ears around, lifted his tail and gave it a good shake. He got up on all fours, gave a deep whine and searched the area. Hopeful. But there was only the big one, squatted down beside his bed, her dress hanging on the floor. A sniff at the bowl but it smelt all wrong. The wrong scent covered the food. This was the little one's aroma. He circled the worn cushion three times, pawed to soften a lump and flopped down with his back to the bowl. With his tail curled around his rump, he dropped his nose onto his paws and closed his eyes to wait. He'd not had water for two days, hadn't eaten, but it wasn't hunger that gnawed away at his innards. Why hadn't he come?

'I'm sorry, Boy. Wish I could explain. Wish you could understand.'

He trailed her sounds with his ears as she rose and padded away back to the kitchen. Normal noises followed. Pans rattled, the oven door opened, the fridge too. Water splashed - dishes echoed from the metal sink. The noises were comforting but didn't ease the deep pain in his innards.

Where was he? Two afternoons now, he hadn't come in. Two mornings now, there'd been no walk down the long drive where he could sniff and explore the sparse shrubs: where he could lift his leg to leave his scent. There had been no ride on the front seat with the window down so he could hang his head out to absorb and enjoy all the scents in the wind. No sticks or birds to chase, no sheep to round up, no treats from the hidden pocket, no pats, no dropped pieces of meat under the table. No nothing. No Grandpa.

The little one pelted though the back entry, her excited voice echoing even before the bang of the door as it bounced from the wall. Relief at the familiar voices eased the pain a little. A brief period of normality brought calm and renewed hope. Grandpa usually came in not long after the little one. Eager to greet him at the back door, Boy rose, lapped at the water bowl to ease his thirst and bounded along the short passage. He rounded the doorway and stood in front of the little one who sat at the table. She smiled, dropped her hand with a sweet biscuit held between her fingers, waved it at him. He edged forwards, sniffed and wrapped his lips around the treat. Hungry, he swallowed it whole as he trotted to the closed door and sat.

Boy dropped to his haunches and whined with his nose high. When nothing happened, he twisted his head, eyeballed the big one and yipped.

'What's wrong with him?' asked the little one.

'I think he's pining for Grandpa. He hasn't eaten.'

The little one giggled. 'He just ate my biscuit.'

'At least it's something but sweet biscuits covered in sugar aren't good for him.' At last, the big one opened the door.

The wind held scents he liked: familiar scents but the strongest came from a pair of boots lined up on the boards. He sniffed and saliva drooled. Maybe if he searched, he'd find Grandpa. Nose to the ground he followed the beloved scent even though it was a bit faint. He repeated the trail he'd taken two days ago. At the first bush, he paused, sniffed, lifted his hind leg and squirted. Relieved, he searched for a fresher trail, found none so followed the old trail back to the boots.

Familiar – the right scent. He squatted on the rough coir mat and panted, stuffed his nose in the gnarled leather. More content, he dropped to his belly with his chin sagged across the boots to wait for the owner: to wait for Grandpa. Soon he will be here.

As he waited, he dozed with one ear pricked, alert for the right footsteps. When the chill of darkness seeped under his fur, he rose and shook. The ache of hunger took hold. He put his nose to the ground and trotted, pausing long enough to leave his mark on another bush as he searched for the meaty bone he'd been given before Grandpa disappeared. Because it was too raw he had buried it. Now, the meat had ripened, making it easy to find. With claws spread wide he pawed at the ground, scraped away the red earth and grasped one end of the bone between his teeth. A gentle tug and it came free. To make sure the meat was ready, he dropped the bone, sniffed and licked. Happy, he wrapped his teeth around the middle and trotted back to the boots. Front paws held the bone while he gnawed, stripping all the flesh and gulping it down. Hunger sated, he stretched on the mat with his nose over the boots and slept.

Heat from the sun had dried up the night damp by the time stirrings came from inside. Boy stretched and left the warmth of the mat to find a place to relieve the pressure of last night's meal. On his way back to the boots, he paused when the door opened and out came the big one and little one, both dressed in the clothes they wore when they disappeared for a long time and came back with overflowing bags. He sat and whined.

'Boy, where have you been?' said the big one.

He cocked his head to one side, tongue lolling from the edge of his mouth, and stared.

'Maybe we can sneak him in,' said the little one.

'What? No way. They wouldn't let a dog inside.'

'But he's so sad and lonely. Maybe if he sees, he will understand. Grandpa would want it.'

Grandpa. At the right word, Boy padded closer, sat, lifted his head and stared.

'Look at his eyes, pleading. Okay, get his lead, we'll give it a go.'

The little one squealed and ran, returning with Boy's lead. At the sight, he stood and swept his tail from side to side. The little one led him to the wrong vehicle but he leapt on the rear seat and shuffled over when she climbed in next to him. Even though he left a trail of moisture on the glass, it didn't go down so he could get his head out. Frustrated, he finally dropped his belly to the smooth, cold seat and pressed his snout on his front paws with his eyes on the little one until the hum of the engine stopped.

Boy leapt out, stood and shook. Weaving his head from side to side, he sniffed but didn't like the scents. The little one tugged on his collar. He followed but baulked at the door to the building. The scents on the other side were like the place where sharp things were jabbed into his scruff. The door opened. The scents overwhelmed him. The little one tugged until the collar tightened so much he couldn't breathe.

'Come on, Grandpa would want this.' At the magic word from the little one, he crept forward, hunched low, ears twitching, eyes swinging – down a long passage, chairs along each side. He resisted the urge to growl but whined instead – a soft whine of fear. He didn't like this place. Danger lurked. He quickened his step, slunk against the familiar legs of the little one and trotted next to her feet. They paused at a door. The door opened.

Boy sniffed, yipped and his tail whipped from side to side so hard his backside followed. His feet scrabbled at the ground, trying to find traction on the slippery floor. He couldn't help the excited leak before he took off and leapt – up – onto the bed where he licked the beloved face. A big familiar hand crept under his collar and scritched. Long splayed fingers ran down his spine to ease the ache. Hands came either side of his face and rubbed. He spread his lips in a smile of joy.

'Hey, Boy. What's this I hear about you not eating?'

Boy nosed into the chest, sniffed and licked, absorbing the aroma and taste. He lay along the legs, dropped his head on his front paws and stared. Grandpa.

The Loveliest and Best
'… I will be your witness …'
Graham Chapman

XXI. Lo! some we loved, <u>the loveliest and the best</u>
That Time and Fate of all their Vintage prest,
Have drunk their Cup a Round or two before,
And one by one crept silently to Rest.

Omar Khayyam

Harold paid for his coffee and lifted his keep cup off the ledge. The protective band was missing so he used his handkerchief to hold the hot cup. While he had other cups, this one reminded him of walking New York with *the loveliest and best*.

They'd walked the High Line and climbed into the Vessel and then had coffee at the Blue Bottle. She went shopping while he sat and got into a conversation with a man from a different culture. Just one of many priceless experiences that happened because he was with *the loveliest and best*.

After a few sips of his coffee, he walked towards the jetty and began a slow amble out over the still clear water. There was no wind, and the morning was mild and fine. He was in a comfortable place for grieving.

It had been six weeks now and he felt an emptiness different to any sort of emptiness he had ever felt before. She was *the loveliest and best* and he missed her wisdom, her comfort, her challenge and a host of other things. Whilst he could recount and list lots of things about her that he missed, it was her unique presence, *the loveliest and best,* that was his greatest loss.

He had escaped south for walks along wild beaches and through tall trees and around calm rivers. These experiences, along with the superb local red wine and good food, had facilitated a journey into himself of deep and meandering reflection. He had gifted himself ample time to just *be* and wasn't in a hurry for the next stage of his life. However, he knew it loomed ahead and couldn't be avoided, especially as he was a *witness* to *the loveliest and best.*

Craftily he had sent texts and photos to the concerned family of his journey to reassure them he was alive and well. They had left him alone.

Alive. That's what had happened to him thanks to her, *the loveliest and best.* He would delight in being a *witness to the loveliest and best.*

Footprints
Dianne Morton

Tiny footprints weave their way along the shore.
The sun rises slowly from beyond the dunes.
The ocean shimmers in the early morning light.

She shivers in the morning chill.
She watches the tide wash the tiny footprints away.
And waits, until the sand is washed clean.

Alone on the beach in the dawn of a new day.
Tiny footprints weave their way along the shore.
She weeps as the tide washes the footprints away.

She sees the footprints that are not there.
And remembers a little girl laughing.
Leaving tiny footprints indented in the sand.

Tears flow, a gentle hand rests on her shoulder.
She turns away from the incoming tide.
Away from the rising sun that warms the sand.

Bat Stew
Victoria Mizen

Once upon a time in a village far, far away, an old woman lived in a tumbledown cottage with her cat.

Children in the village liked to play tricks on her, dropping things like frogs, lizards and spiders through the cracks in her front door. They picked the flowers off her medicinal herbs and the roses off her bushes, throwing them into the street. They particularly enjoyed shouting rude words at her then running away before she could respond.

The old woman wore a long black cape over her ragged black clothes. A pointy black hat was perched on her head, only partly covering the wispy strands of grey hair. A broom was frequently seen on her verandah and strange noises were often heard from her house, especially around midnight, when any good woman should be sound asleep.

The children in the village were sure she was a witch, especially after young Morris saw her stirring smelly hot liquid in the copper in her back yard. He reported hearing her saying over and over, something that sounded like a spell as she stirred. The words were foreign, but everyone knew that she came from another country.

Elizabeth, one of the village children, loved cats. Despite the fear that all the others felt towards the old woman, she sometimes crept into her back garden at night, bringing treats like a rabbit's ear or the wing of a dead bird, to the cat who purred her appreciation and tolerated the girl's stroking.

Several years went by, Elizabeth grew into a beautiful, charming young woman, who all the boys for miles around wanted to claim as a wife. None of them liked the fact that she befriended the old woman's cat, but they were willing to ignore this slight fault.

Until one moonless night when the cat led Elizabeth into the old woman's house via an open window. The old woman was startled by the girl's arrival, but as her cat had accepted Elizabeth, she was tempted to do the same. Given the treats that were offered to her cat, the old woman thought Elizabeth might appreciate a bowl of her stew. Soon her visitor was seated at her table, daintily sipping on the odd smelling, but tasty brew.

'May I ask what's in your recipe?' Elizabeth enquired when the bowl was almost empty.

The old woman hesitated but eventually responded with another question. 'Oh, do you like my bat stew?'

Elizabeth leapt up, flung the bowl on the floor, and ran out of the woman's house.

Picking up her cat, the old woman stroked her. 'Clever pussy,' she said. 'You like the flavour of bats, but what makes that silly girl think I would eat them. Sorry about your treats, but I think we will now be rid of pesky visitors. She will convince them all that I'm definitely a witch and should be avoided.'

Grandmother's Reward
Janusz Zejdler

A grandmother and her grandson shared a unique bond in a small village: a village where the average residency comprised a small holding of land from which the family made a living. There was acreage for sowing and gathering, a nearby garden for vegetables and orchards for fruit. One or two cows, a horse and a mix of poultry completed the wholesome living style. These resources varied depending on those who were more ambitious and those who survived from day to day.

In one of these homes lived a grandmother alone; her husband left for eternal rest, and the children also moved away as farming could not sustain all of them. Some grandchildren visited her from time to time, more a holiday for them, and a mix of responses for the grandmother. They offered help with the not-too-complex activities, those more of a nuisance, like digging the garden, feeding the cow, or taking it to pasture. There was no question of them doing the harder tasks like picking apples off the trees or chopping the wood. They provided a bit of company. Despite the challenges, the grandmother's resilience inspired those around her.

Being constantly alone and caring for the land and animals was demanding. The weekly church gathering provided group activities and gossip about what had happened in the village. Occasional visits from the local Vicar broke up the routine, and one of the villager's news providers (gossiper) kept her up to date with everything that took place in the village, the good, the bad, and the very private.

And so, the life of the aging grandmother went on.

One of her grandsons, a young, innocent boy, visited her during his school holidays. He was slow and took his time to carry out tasks. Once, when asked to clear weeds in the vegetable plot, he took his time. He was doing everything else instead of what he was asked to do. It irritated the grandmother; she wanted things done and done quickly. He would work when she was there, but when she left, he went back to time-wasting. After a few reminders, she lost her temper, grabbed the hoe from his hands and tried to push him away from the vegetable plot, but as he ducked away from her, he received a hit on the back of his head. In his innocence, the boy grabbed his head and fell to his knees.

Not paying attention to the boy, she quickly moved to her chores. When the evening meal came, there was no sign of the boy. Knowing his slow and ill-considered behaviour, she didn't give too much concern about him. When it turned dark, and there was still no sign of him, she went out to look. She was most surprised by his absence — it should have been enough that she looked after him. She shouldn't have to lead him by the hand like a tiny baby.

After a while, she found him where she had left him. But this time, he was no longer on his knees but flat on his face and not moving. She panicked, not knowing what to do. She tried to turn him on his back and wake him. When this failed, she froze with the thought that she may have killed him. There was no one close by to seek help. Feeling useless, she returned to the house, trying to decide what to do next. Still unsettled, she went outside, walked past a drum that was three-quarters full of cow feed liquid mixture. She recalled the grandson's daily task to mix this with other food. She stood there for a while and, with a chilling expression, hurried to where the grandson was.

The following day, she was up with the sunrise and went outside to find her grandson halfway in the drum, headfirst. Her efforts to pull him out failed. She ran to the village, screaming to report what she saw. The doctor and the village sheriff attended. Their initial inspection concluded that the boy, attempting to feed the cow, overbalanced and fell into the barrel. The position he found himself in prevented him from getting out, and he drowned in the thick mix.

The body was cleaned, the thick mix removed and the doctor examined him closer, only to find a spot on the back of the boy's head, which aroused suspicion. Was it drowning, or was it an intended hit?

This led to the sheriff arresting the grandmother on suspicion of homicide. It meant that an autopsy was to be conducted to determine the cause of death. The autopsy results concluded that the boy's death was by drowning. The strike on the head only caused a temporary loss of consciousness. The conclusion is that the boy was still alive when put into the barrel of the cow's food. Trying to breathe, he sucked the thick mixture into his air passage and blocked the intake of air to the lungs. It resulted in his death. There were no other people close to the grandmother's farm who might have done this. In conclusion, she alone was responsible for the grandson's death by placing him in the barrel headfirst. It was murder.

The police from the town were called in to take over the case. One police officer arrived with a rifle and handcuffs. The local sheriff passed on all the gathered information relating to this case. The grandmother was officially charged with murder, cuffed with her hands in front of her and a chain attached to the police officer. He lead her through the village the city jail, where further action was taken. She looked so small and almost worthy of sympathy for the way she was treated.

This one unintended act weighed against all the good she had previously done. A life that was not easy, to bring up a family, and the good she did for the village and those in need. The family left her without any support or guidance. They'd send her grandchildren not to help her but to get rid of them so they could have a rest from them.

She has paid the price for them.

My Nicole
Nicole Corsini

I remember the first time we met. Her little face lit up when the bearded man she called, Dad, handed me over. She squeezed me so hard I thought my stitching might burst at the seams.

'Mum, look what I got! I'm going to name her Misty,' she exclaimed to the lady next to her. I knew she loved me from that moment and I loved her back. I was hers and she was mine.

The other people in the house called my little girl, Nicole. We did everything together. I was there for the fun times, but more important, I was there for the hard times, when she needed me most.

My scruffy brown fur absorbed hundreds of shed tears. My long floppy ears stored countless words of her feelings, secrets and fears. I told her I loved her every day and would never hurt her the way the world does sometimes. She couldn't hear me but I know she knew.

Not long after I was given a dog family of my own, four adopted children to be exact. We all had a place in Nicole's bed, lined up biggest to smallest. I was always number one. The start of the line. The closest to her.

As she grew there was less room in the bed. Nicole made us a dog kennel out of a cardboard box, we spent hours together on it. She did the making and I told her how good it looked. We got a warm blanket to sleep on and a little bowl in the corner filled with water. Snuggled in and positioned in our orderly line, I stayed with my dog family in the cardboard kennel, next to the bed.

It wasn't as cosy as I was used to and I missed Nicole terribly. She must have felt the same because a few hours into the night I was lifted out and tucked into her bed. It was nice, just the two of us.

The next morning I was reunited with my puppies in the kennel and we were given a bowl of real dog biscuits. I can't tell you how much I wished I could have eaten those biscuits for her.

'Have a good day all of you and I will be back straight after school.' We were all given a pat on the head before she left the room. I waited patiently still, exactly where she put me until she returned home from school again.

As time went by, Nicole was able to sleep the whole night without bringing me into her bed. My little girl didn't need me so much anymore.

Things really started to change on the day of her eleventh birthday sleep over party. She was so excited when she took me and my dog family out of our cardboard home where we had sat for quite some time, untouched, apart from the water bowl that had been refreshed every so often. I thought, she wants us to join the party, how exciting!

But we weren't being played with this time.

I'd seen many teddies and toys go into the toy box over the years but never thought I would be one of them. My family members maybe, but not me. One by one we were put inside the pink fabric-covered box, with more care than the other toys but it hurt all the same. The lid closed, leaving me in darkness. I didn't know darkness could be so painful.

I was blind to the world but I could hear Nicole and her four girlfriends in the room. Muffled voices came through the fabric walls of my cell. There were giggles and talk of cute boys and the mean girl from school that none of them liked. I wanted to join the conversation and tell her friends that I had heard about Mean Tammy many times too.

The toy box became my new home and eventually was traded for an oversized old brown suitcase. A few of the stuffed toys didn't make the cut, the rest of us lucky ones were pushed and shoved into the suitcase. Nicole had to lay on top of it to be able to zip it all the way up.

'Mum, these are the ones I'm keeping. Where can I put them?' The voice travelled into the suitcase. We may not have been played with anymore, but we were being kept at least, I had to be thankful for that.

'I'll put it in the shed,' Mum replied.

In total silence and darkness, days and nights rolled into one quick seven years. I stayed the same while, outside, Nicole grew taller, bigger, older. When the zip finally opened, I wasn't prepared for what I saw. Blinded by the sudden light, it took a few moments for my eyes to adjust to this girl who now held me in her hands.

'Aww, my teddies! I forgot all about them.' The young woman was excited to see me. A nostalgic smile filled her face as she brushed at my fur. I couldn't tell if it was for comfort or to remove dust that had managed to enter the isolation box. I told myself it was the first.

'Do you want to keep them? I'm clearing out the shed so if you don't want them they will have to go,' Mum told Nicole.

'Yes I definitely want them, but I have nowhere to put them right now. Can they stay there until I find somewhere please?' I knew she would never get rid of me.

She must not have been able to find somewhere quick enough because the next thing I knew I was inside a warehouse being dumped onto a giant pile of other stuffed animals, all of them strangers.

I spotted my dog family as they tumbled in different directions on the pile. Human hands reached in and started sorting us into hessian bags with no apparent order. Not a single one of my family were bagged with me, I wondered if that was the last time we would be together.

Back in darkness, the bag journeyed through hands, trucks, more hands until I was settled into a basket on a shelf in a store. There was a sign above that read *Pre-Loved Toys $5*. There's something about that word – pre-loved, like you were once loved but no longer loved any more. Surely that wasn't me.

The next thirteen years were a blur. New homes came and went. New children loved me then didn't. The environments changed but I remained the same.

My last journey was the biggest surprise. After my owner, a boy called Ben, had grown and my purpose once again complete, I wasn't donated like the other times. Ben's mum took my photo and put it on something called Ebay.com. There was no pre-loved sign, instead she wrote *Vintage Plush Toy Puppy Dog*. That title sounded much nicer to me, like I was something worth having.

Off to my next adventure I travelled alone, tightly squeezed into yet another bag. Car to plane. Plane to van. Van to house. Through many different hands.

'It's here!' A lady's voice came through the bag before it was excitedly torn open.

There she was my new owner. Aged by time but still exactly the same. My Nicole.

A little hand reached up and stroked my vintage fur.

'What's that Mum?' a childish voice asked.

'This is my Misty. It was my favourite teddy in the whole world when I was a kid. It was given away at some point when I thought I didn't need teddies anymore. But I've been looking in op-shops and online for it for so many years and finally found it. I'm so unbelievably happy.' She squeezed me just like she had before.

'Is it for me?' The little voice was hopeful.

Nicole let out a little laugh, I had missed that sound more than I knew. 'No, not this one. This is just for me. Sorry, I'm never letting it go ever again.'

That night I laid still, wrapped in the arms of my favourite person. Where I was meant to be all along.

Staying Afloat
Janelle Macgregor

I was cast into the sea in a storm just like the one that's coming now. Four months ago, it was. I'm not as anxious as I was then because I've been through turbulent weather a few times since.

The people who threw me into the water were refugees from somewhere. Even before the storm, they were in difficulties with sick children and almost no fresh water. The turbulence eventually pushed them towards an island, or an isthmus, that wasn't on their map. As the wind and water began to settle, they estimated they could reach the beach using damaged timbers as rafts. It was worth the risk to them to find fresh water and food on firm land, rather than float around on a wreck of a boat. Before leaving, they wrote down their coordinates and a few details, sealed the paper into me, and overboard I went. I was a good choice. My glass is clear and dense, my base is wide and solid, and my neck is tall and narrow. They thought I would float well, and so I have.

Since I've been in the water I've been flipped in the air by dolphins, nuzzled lovingly by whales, and curtly nudged along by sharks. I've been pecked at by birds of all shapes and sizes and, once on a very still day, a young gull used me as a resting place. Seaweed is a bit of a hazard, but rocks or reefs are my greatest danger. So far, the current has kept me drifting around the ocean and away from land. A couple of times I've found myself in shipping lanes or amongst fishing fleets and I've come close to being run down more than once. Unfortunately, for my refugee families, no one has spotted me and scooped me up.

After these four months, I know when bad weather is approaching. The first thing that happens is I find myself alone. The mammals and big fish disappear first. The small fish follow. When dawn broke this morning, the birds had gone, too, and there was no noise – no fish jumping, no albatross winging, no wave curling in upon itself. Silence. Calm.

An hour later, the sea began to swell; very large ripples on a very large pond developed into small undulating hillocks for as far as I could see. In the next hour I could feel a surge from deep down beneath me and, at the same time, the sky dulled to a patchy watercolour of greys, with cumulus gathering above the western horizon.

The undercurrent began to tug at me. I rolled onto my side and remained as steady as I could in the increasing swell. The rain became intense, so heavy that I feared it might push me under, so I bounced back to upright.

Soon, the clouds were flooding in my direction. The greys and whites added indigoes and purples and deep tones of green, as they stumbled upon themselves. The waves began to heave, and the thunder rolled in. Lightning flashed. Lightning flared. A forest of lightning above me.

Now the waves are tossing, and their crests are breaking around me. Hills and valleys. Valleys and mountains. Summits and trenches. I rise on the surge then I'm pitched into the ditch. Up, down. Up, down. Twisting, spinning. Somersaulting. And there is so much noise now. Tumult.

The thunder wanes, but the wind still seethes. The wind wails. The wind gusts the clouds across the top of me. I've lost my bearings. I can't tell the direction the storm is taking, only that the lightning is becoming less dense directly above me and is moving beyond me.

I dare to hope that the worst has passed. I feel some relief, but I realize the elements are far from settled. The cresting and collapsing continues. A faint light peeks through on the horizon; a little light on one side of me, a lot of darkness on the other.

I can't tell how much time has passed but I sense it's been several hours. Could it be a day? For however long the storm has raged, I've only been concerned with the next wave. Now I'm feeling fretful. Might this storm be the start of a seasonal change with many more storms to come? How much battering will my seal take? How many times can I be thrashed from the pinnacle of a wave into the solid gully below without breaking?

The lightning is receding into the distance. The light I'd noticed to the other side of me, now has the glow of a sunset. The wind is easing from gale-force, and the white caps have stopped swirling. I am still rising and falling. Falling and rising. A rhythm. The wind is pulsating to the rhythm of the sea.

The refugee families may have been discovered by now. They may have been taken to freedom; they may have been taken to detention. Or they may be lost and lingering where I left them. Perhaps, I'll never know their fate. But I have a responsibility to them to stay afloat for as long as I can.

When the sea is more relaxed, tomorrow, the next day, I will daydream again. I will imagine that the sun is sparkling off me, and a passing vessel will see me. A passing vessel will see me and spoon me up from the ocean. Then, the secret I hold will be released.

The Polly Caper
Garry Davies

Most of my marks are real animals. A low-life will go missing, and someone — it's usually a woman — will be sitting opposite my desk with pleading eyes and a quivering voice. That's what I do: I look for the kind the police aren't interested in finding. I'm not too self-righteous about the system, if the police don't care, then I do. It's a service, but it's not free. I'll find anything, as long as it's lost and there's money in it.

Mrs Hillary Josephs said she had the money. Some old bird was missing, gone without a word…

'…and when I got up, Mr Tracey, I didn't hear her call out, I checked her room and she was gone. Her door was open and the bedroom window was broken. I've reported it to the police, but all they seem interested in is the break and enter. No one cares about old Polly going missing.'

'Her name is Polly?'

'Yes.'

'Let me see if I've got this.' Mrs Josephs, now divorced, nodded and I continued. 'Black, female, elderly, a bit talkative, long nails, called Polly. Found to be missing yesterday morning, possible break and enter during the previous night. No known friends. No other known hangouts.' She nodded again. But I needed another angle, some old sticky-beak doesn't get herself stolen for no reason. Maybe she's dead? Maybe it's just that the body hasn't turned up yet? And why does this woman care about the old bird? She's a working-class girl who doesn't have money to waste — her crumpled nylon dress and balled-up cardigan tell their own story.

'Why do you want to spend the money, Mrs Josephs?' Her knuckles whitened as she worked the screwed-up handkerchief a little more; her voice was strained.

'I … I love Polly, Mr Tracey. I just want her back.'

'I'll come to your place and have a look around.'

'No, don't! There's no need for you to come. I've told you everything.' She looked genuine, but in my business that's often the time to start digging further.

'Is she worth anything, Mrs Josephs? Has anyone tried to take her before? Anyone been hanging around?'

'No, no. Nothing like that.'

And that was that. She left her phone number and address, with a promise of a cash deposit to come later.

My first move was to ring Dale Fairweather of the RSPCA Enforcement Section. A missing red-tailed black cockatoo doesn't just vanish, and Fairweather was a good woman to know. For lots of reasons.

'Dale, babe, how are you? … no, it's Les. … Les Tracey.' She hadn't heard of a missing red tail. She would enter Polly and Mrs Josephs into the database and see what came back. She didn't want to have a drink with me after work and would call me if anything turned up. Fairweather was all business, as usual. I had other hopes. Being Perth's top wildlife retriever isn't as glamorous as it sounds, and sometimes I need to find some human company to ease the pain of the raw animal tragedy that surrounds my daily life. Fairweather wasn't playing ball — yet — but she said she would call.

Athol's shop was one of those older timber-framed, glass-fronted places built right up to the Perth footpath. In the window the mongoose and cobra were locked in mortal combat, forever at the instant before one or the other made the fatal strike. It was the only place I knew where the owl and the pussycat really were together in a pea-green boat. A good taxidermist needs a touch of whimsy, and Athol Mount was a good taxidermist.

'Hello, Athol, stuffed anything living lately?' He loved taxidermist jokes and he appeared to like my company. No-one was in the shop whenever I called by, so he had little choice.

'Piss-off, Tracey, I'm a busy man.' Athol was working on a red fox which was posed with teeth bared, ready to strike.

'I'm looking for a stolen red-tail cockatoo, you haven't had one turn up, have you?'

'No red-tail, but a galah just walked in. Piss-off, Tracey.' I overlooked this further expression of whimsy and pressed on. The snarl on the fox looked real.

'What about a market for it, is there much call for stuffed cockatoos?' He put down his instrument and looked at me. I noticed that the fox didn't take any notice — he hadn't fitted the glass eyes yet.

'I told you before, I don't stuff animals. I preserve them in artistic tableaux of life. Stuffing is what you do to capsicums. And if it was alive when it went missing, it won't be preserved, it'll be smuggled out and sold overseas on the live animal market. The red tail is the rarest of the cockatoos, could be worth thousands.' Athol returned to his work. He always impressed me by what he knew about these things. I took another glance at the fox without eyes and, as I'm a sensitive guy, thought about the symbolism.

I thanked Athol and left. They both pretended not to notice.

I wondered why Dale didn't mention the live animal trade, or the value of the bird. I hoped she would owe me one for that slip.

The window creaked and the lock gave way with a snap. It was an old lift-up sliding sash with a useless catch. Hillary Josephs lived in a duplex-half in Belmont not far from the airport. Cheap land, and a cheap house, yet she said she could afford to pay me to run around town after a missing parrot. I wanted to check her story, something didn't smell right, and after I hoisted up her back window I found what it was. The place was sparsely furnished, a few dishes on the kitchen table,

a small refrigerator, a bed, and a few clothes. In one room, newspapers were over the floor, they were covered with bird droppings and black feathers. And on a table stood an old birdcage with a black cockatoo in it. Either she didn't waste any time getting a replacement, or Polly was back.
One other thing I noticed as I shut the back window. The glass and putty was new.

I returned to my office and called Dale again.

'Dale, babe, how are you?' She was still fine; Hillary Josephs had no priors for smuggling, or any other animal-related crime; there was a huge market for Australian parrots of all species overseas and the red-tail was the most valuable, which she didn't mention because I was supposed to be the detective. I told her about the new parrot at the home in Belmont. She was interested and took down the details. I knew she had a soft spot for me but she still wasn't thirsty. No drink.

Then I spoke to Mrs Josephs' message-bank. I had to pump her about the bird in the cage, without letting on about my break-in.

A day later she paid me a visit. There was a knock at the door, and I ushered Mrs Josephs into a chair. The handkerchief and red eyes were back. I pretended to be surprised about the new parrot missing she spoke of.

'…and now Celeste is missing, Mr Tracey, gone just like Polly.'

This has to be the unluckiest woman in Perth. 'Another bird gone?'

'Yes, and another broken window. The insurance will only pay for one. A single window a year is all they allow.'

I'm not a free public service and the uncomfortable feeling I had about money and Mrs Josephs returned again. I turn people who can't pay away all the time — my bank manager insists. But then she brought out the big one.

'Please, Mr Tracey.' My resolve was almost gone. And I wanted to know about the second red-tail. 'It can't be any more to find two birds instead of one, and I have a little money with me.'

And that was it. I'm sure my bank manager would have needed to see her in new clothes and a hairdo before he gave in.

A day or two passed before I received another call, late in the afternoon, from Mrs Josephs. She wanted to meet me right away at Athol Mount's shop in King Street. She hung up before I could get any more information, but it was intriguing enough for me to drop everything and go. The thud from the everything I dropped wouldn't be loud.

'Hello, Athol, business looks dead!'

'Piss-off, Tracey.' The fox was gone and Athol was working on a new block to cover with a pelt: a small dog or cat, perhaps. He was carefully hollowing out the block to reduce the weight. Then his shop-door opened and in came the transformation that used to be Mrs Josephs, with several of her friends, and a large parcel.

'Mr Tracey, it's time we met properly.' I would have settled for an improper meeting, even with the official blue uniform, the woman was a knockout.

'I'm inspector Hillary Josephs of the Australian Customs Service.' She certainly was. And her friends were all in plainclothes from the WA Police, three of them.

'I have a warrant to search your premises, Mr Mount.' Athol was usually a model of refined behaviour, but now he reacted badly to this news. Even I was caught a little off guard. The three policemen were enough to overcome the temporary lack of decorum Athol displayed, he was soon spread-eagled, face down on his own floor with his hands behind his back, retained by inspector Joseph's handcuffs. She barely raised a puff, and I was growing more impressed by the minute. Even the mongoose and cobra seemed to notice.

'What's this …' was as far as I got when Dale Fairweather came in with another policeman. Athol's shop was getting to be a fairly official place, and I knew something was up in a big way. The police usually weren't this interested in missing animals.

'Mr Mount, have you seen this before?' Athol was pulled to his feet by two of his new friends, he stared in silence as inspector Josephs took the paper wrapping from my old friend the fox — now with eyes. Dale's look could have killed Mount. Athol remained silent.

'Mr Tracey, have you seen this fox before?'

'Well, yes, Athol was working on it Wednesday. I saw it here' I answered. She faced Athol.

'It was, as you know Mr Mount, addressed to an overseas destination. We intercepted it today in the Qantas freight terminal.' She took one of Athol's blades and slashed at the belly, then pulled the fur away from the hollow foam block underneath. She lifted a large cover cut into the block.
'Still nothing to say, Mr Mount?' Inside was a wire cage containing what I guessed to be the now found, but obviously drugged, Polly.

'Under police supervision, this bird has been implanted with a micro-chip. It can be proven to be the cockatoo known as Celeste and seen by Mr Tracey in a residence in Belmont three days ago. Mr Tracey is that correct?,' inspector Josephs asked me.

'Ah, yes. Yes. That's the bird I saw.' Polly or Celest. who knows? I'm sure the po? e tag would show which one it was, and this didn't seem to be the time to say that all red-tailed black cockatoos look alike — or to ask how she knew about my break-in.

Dale looked shaken. Like most members of the RSPCA, her work was more than a job.

But then a new twist to this tale. 'Ms Dale Fairweather,' inspector Josephs turned to face Dale. The policeman she entered with took Dale's arm. 'I arrest you as an accessory to Athol Mount in exporting live native fauna.'

I guessed immediately that Dale wasn't as dedicated as I thought.

Inspector Hillary hasn't said if there ever was a Polly. But Dale Fairweather and I were the only ones who knew about Celeste. Hillary said things looked bad for both Dale and me, but when they recorded Dale calling Mount about the new red-tail, which cleared me and shopped the pair of them.

I never did get to have that drink with Dale. And neither will anyone else for the next few years. I'll manage to get over her with some help from Hillary, who's been giving me bird identification lessons on weekends. As for Athol, I like the symbolism of a fox being stuffed by a live parrot. I can only hope that the other jailbirds don't have the same sense of whimsey.

A Thief in the Night
Su Watson

I came like a thief in the night, no fanfare, no parade, and you welcomed me with open arms. With hugs and handshakes, you helped me to settle in quickly, introducing me around like a long-lost relative. At first, we weren't sure how you'd take to me. Being a newcomer is always a bit of a gamble, but we needn't have worried. Your surety about your place in the scheme of things gave you the belief that there was nothing to fear. Without your supreme confidence, I'd never have set up a network that would carry me across borders, across oceans.

Of course, that self-esteem, that arrogance, is why I'm here. An adjustment needs to be made, the rectification of a mistake. It's obvious now, as things so often are in hindsight, you should never have been allowed to climb down from the trees. Who could have known you'd come this far, this quickly? You just don't seem to know when to stop. The more powerful you become, the more entitled, and with your entitlement, balance is being pushed further and further aside.

Over the centuries we've tried to keep you in check — a drought here, a flood there, a famine, a plague. Each time, instead of learning that you are just one player who cannot win the game without the entire team, you bounce back with a vengeance, more determined than ever to subvert the rules and fix the match in your favour. How many animals are gone now, how many forests decimated, oceans polluted, other creatures squeezed into less and less space? But it's all the same to you, isn't it? You believe you were made in the image of God, and so are more special, more important than everything else. I do wonder, though, why you think the rest of creation is here. Has it never once occurred to you that maybe we were all made in God's image and that together, we make up the perfect whole? Obviously not, otherwise you wouldn't keep making the same mistakes. An economy based on perpetual growth is simply not sustainable. So, we've decided to step in before you deplete the resource beyond repair, and there's only you left.

Hence the thief in the night. We knew we had to move quickly. Once the secret was out, once you knew I was not as harmless as I appeared, we knew you'd move to shut me down. You're nothing if not adaptable. A true definition of a medical virus, if ever there was one. At the moment, you're bunkered down, restricting movement, staying as far from each other as possible, but experience tells us it won't last. Soon you'll tire of the restrictions. You haven't come this far to be cowed by some invisible pathogen. Your sense of birthright will reassert itself. So, a few old folks, a few sick people, will die. 'Isn't that the way it goes?' you'll say. After all, it's your ruthlessness, your willingness to sacrifice even your own kind, that's made you so successful. With a shrug, you'll justify the wellbeing of the economy over the health of the community, as though it's some sacred beast. Of course, you imagine that somehow you and yours will be saved.

Yes, we know about your plans for the vaccines. I must admit you were on to that quicker than we expected. Greed slowed you down, but you did at least recognise the threat. Even now, you're trying to keep up with me. As I shimmer and change and slip through your net, you still believe in your illusion of control. And while you're focussing on me, my teammates are getting ready for another push forward. We contemplated waiting until you destroyed yourselves, but decided it was too risky. Too many of the rest of us will fall before you. So, you should know, we aren't coming for your old, or you're sick, we're coming for you. Time to shove the genie back in the bottle before it's too late.

Students' Racist Slurs Outrage Community
Cynthia Fenton

I was appalled, as many locals were, at the tirade of racist slurs and obscenities hurled at a young, female (Asian) ALDI supermarket manager by a mob of students from a Kalamunda high school recently.

Local Facebook groups were outraged, with a multitude of comments saying everything from: 'its only kids from the foothills, it's the teachers' fault, the location of the bus station, or we need a police station.' Well, that old chestnut did not curb juvenile crime so it was removed.

The following Friday morning I decided to call out the reprehensible behaviour at ALDI. Initially on my own, two dads soon joined me, as I explained to students that they were unable to enter ALDI because their disgraceful behaviour did not represent the values of my community.

I received a bit of cheek. One student, pacing up and down the front steps, continued his intimidation. I stood my ground knowing other mums had dropped by the store or phoned to check on the victim's welfare.

While verbal assault is not a crime, (in Western Australia); the manager is within her rights to take her case to the Australian Human Rights Commission (AHRC). An ALDI manager last week said, 'The police, ALDI and the school have addressed the issue with the help of closed-circuit television (CCTV) and the police have supported ALDI's move to ban students…from their premises…'

One can only hope the parents of the offending students are involved. Moreover, herein lays the challenge: unprovoked attacks by teenage boys exhibit aggression because it is learned. Sure, we can blame the old *cliché* —these boys are victims of emotional, physical, or sexual violence at home. This is not an excuse.

Kalamunda's community has witnessed some teens who are unable to control their emotions, and hate, fuelled by perceived powerlessness encouraged by misogynistic social media. Most of our school students generally demonstrate excellent Vocational Education, and Australian Tertiary Admission Rank results. Many contribute to our community in a myriad of positive ways.

However, holding them to account is everyone's job. Educators already teach and guide our kids. Police have bigger fish to fry and resist arresting kids, admitting that juvenile detention is a dead end. If mums protest in public it makes our kids ripe for bullying — another headache for school administration.

Boys need to see real male power, courageous role models. Girls, too, need to witness men call out racism and sexism, and reinforce that they deserve much, much better. Outrage on Facebook is fine, but comments come and go — they bring the heat in as fast as it sizzles out.

I believe Australia's challenge in this decade is our moral compass. Everyone, and particularly men, can step up at our shared spaces and say, 'Kids you cannot stay here today, we do not accept racism and abuse'. Are we ready to put our ideals where our mouth is? Will you step forward when you overhear aggressive, intimidating, and filthy language in public?

It takes a village to raise a child. My shire is that village: a diverse community who stands strong, proud, and leads by example. Let us advocate for our digital era generation before it is too late and they become a real reason for a new police station. Let us say *no more*. Not on my bus, not on my street, not at my pool, my playground or skate park — and never again in my supermarket.

Published online by **The Independent Australia**. March 21st, 2021.

No Regrets
Alwena Willis

Looking at her dead uncle, the knife still in him, the blood sticky around his abdomen and the rug below him. His face was somewhat contorted in death, bringing back those long-ago memories which she had tried so hard to suppress. She had been Maddie's age when he forced himself on her and afterwards when she told her parents. No one had believed her; they believed the lies he had spun instead. She had lived with the shame all her life while he had swanned off to the United States to live what sounded like a fabulous life. She had got over it with the help of the man who became her wonderful husband, but she had never forgiven the perpetrator or her parents really, for believing him. When she saw his photos and his smirk, it tormented her and she wondered how many other girls he had put through the horror he had put her through.

Her mind flashed back to earlier this evening when she got back from the shops to hear Maddie's muffled screams. She hastily placed the shopping on the kitchen bench and saw a man pinning her daughter down on the lounge floor, tearing at her clothes.

Her mind snapped and she screamed, 'No, not my Maddie!'

Unconsciously, she grabbed a knife from the kitchen and rushed at him, pull him off her and stabbed him without a second thought. She saw instantly who it was and the nausea rose in her throat almost overcoming her. Maddie was hysterical, eyes shut tight.

Abbey reached out and held her tight. 'It's alright Maddie it's Mum, keep your eyes closed, Sweetheart. You're safe now.'

With that she pulled Maddie up and guided her to her bedroom. 'Maddie, my hit must have knocked the wind out of him and he has run off, I will get you settled and we will ring the police.'

'Please don't, Mum. I don't want anyone to know. He's gone so shall we just leave it. Dad is back home tomorrow. Please?'

'Okay, Darling,' said Abbey, knowing from experience hr daughter would react like this. She, herself, had only wanted her parents to know and no one else when it happened to her. If they had believed her, they would not be in this mess tonight. Thank goodness she had got here before he had a chance to do anything too serious.

'Pop in the shower, Sweetheart and you can sleep with me tonight. How's that?'

'Yea please, Mum.'

Abbey went downstairs and prepared a mug of warm milk, crushing two sleeping tablets into it. She needed Maddie to sleep heavily tonight. She stayed with her until she was fast asleep and then came back down to face the music.

Now here she was staring at her dead uncle's face. No time to dwell on the past now. Time for action. Her adrenalin kicked in. There was no way she would call the police as it wasn't self-defence, even though she did it to defend Maddie. She would most certainly get a jail sentence. There was no way this man was going to ruin her life twice.

Their home was situated on the estuary and they had a boathouse which housed a small motorboat they used to fish and go craypot fishing. She knew instantly what to do. She pulled the knife out of her uncle, washed it clean, wrapped it in paper and went out and got the wheelbarrow. She brought it inside and used all her strength to wrap her uncle in the rug and roll him into the up-ended barrow, along with the knife, and covered them with a few black plastic bags. Wheeling it in the dark down to the boathouse was difficult but she managed. She placed plastic bags on the floor of the boat and tipped him onto the plastic. More black plastic went over him with several cray pots on top. She hosed the wheelbarrow out, took it back up the garden and filled it with a couple of bags of compost. Back inside she mopped the living room floor with floor cleaner and bleach even though the blood had not seeped through the rug. She then checked on Maddie who was still in a deep sleep and stripped her clothes and showered. Downstairs, she put a load of washing on including her and Maddie's clothes they wore that night and slipped into bed next to Maddie for a couple of hours' sleep.

The alarm woke her at 4.30. She was so tired after barely three hours sleep but the adrenalin kicked in again with a surge. She got out of bed, checked Maddie was still in a deep sleep, dressed, slipped out of the house and made her way down to the boathouse.

Behind the wheel of the boat, she turned on the engine and slowly guided the boat along the estuary and out to sea. She had made this trip with Jack several times to set the cray pots out, so she was confident and soon she was far enough out to feel comfortable that she could not be seen even in the dusk of the morning. She slowly moved the clay pots aside along with the black plastic bags. With the swimming platform lowered, she was able to roll the body to the edge and just let it fall into the sea.

There was no remorse as she watched the body sink. This man her, mother's brother, raped her when she was fourteen and he had no regrets. Yesterday he had full intentions of doing the same to her daughter. No, she had no regrets and no remorse in what she had done though she wished life had been different.

She lifted up the swimming platform and once again behind the wheel of the boat, guided it to their normal cray pot fishing area where she lowered her pots and then leisurely drove the boat home. At home she gathered all the plastic bags she used, quietly set them alight, watched them melt away. The remnants were buried in her garden. She then scrubbed the deck of the boat even though there was no blood that she could see. She didn't want to take any chances. She took another shower, changed once again, made herself a coffee and slowly sipped it watching a new day begin.

Mid-morning Maddie woke.

'Want to go shopping?' Abbey asked as if nothing had happened the night before.

'Sure.' said Maddie, though she looked a bit down. 'What for?'

'A new rug and some cushion covers. I chucked the others away as I want the living room to look different, what do you say.'

Maddie looked at her mum and nodded. 'Great let's go and have some fun; bags I choose the colour.'

Abbey laughed. 'Fine.' She would have given Maddie the world as long as it made her smile again.

Jack came home at 4.00pm to a new lounge which made him smile. 'You girls, I can't leave for three days and come home to a new lounge though I must say it's looking good, what's for tea?'

'Crayfish, I went out early this morning and set them up and Maddie and I are not long back from getting them and we got two beauties.'

Just then Abbey's phone rang. It was her Mum, 'Abbey, Dad and I will come around tomorrow if that's all right and can we bring your uncle Steve with us. He's holidaying from the US at the moment. I know you don't get on with him but you're an adult now and after all family is family. Can we? He said he really would like to see you'

Abbey listened and thought her mother had never understood or believed her but this was a good opportunity.

'Sure Mum, I would love to see him. After all, as you said, we are all grown-ups now. Do you all want to come for tea.

Is there anything in particular you know Uncle Steve likes to eat?'

'Oh, how thoughtful of you, Abbey. Anything seafood really. You know he just loves the sea. I have always thought he is the happiest is when he is in the ocean.'

This comment left Abbey speechless as she dwelt a moment on what she had done and somehow a bubble of dark humour entered her brain which she knew deep down was wrong, so said she had to go and she would see them all tomorrow.

Web Of Lies
Dianne Morton

Beyond the doorway, a spider lies in wait. Waiting for the next victim. Her door is open, welcoming. Enter at your own risk, for life will never be the same afterwards. A dire warning, but some were willing to ignore it, just for the chance of gaining a better life beyond their wildest dreams. Many a gullible person had stood on her doorstep before taking the final plunge inside. To a world beyond reality, living the dream. Trapped in a web of lies. That is until she grew tired of her game and spat out the victims, sending them back to the grimy pavement amongst the rubbish. There they stood destitute, broken-hearted and alone once more. She had a heart of stone that felt nothing for her victims, for she was the Black Widow.

The money he earned; he threw away on the horses. A fool's errand that soon saw him lost without the fortune he felt was his due. Eventually, he had a win, then greed found him and held him in a powerful grip where there was no way he could break free. Until there was no money left that he could hold in his grubby hands. Greed wasn't done with him yet. He wanted; he needed more money to bet his life away on the horses. In a futile search to find more cash to feed his insatiable hunger he crossed paths with the black widow. He came to her door after he lost everything to the world of gambling.

She welcomed him in, a new victim. He wanted money, she wanted to make a fortune. An unlikely and dangerous partnership. One that was destined for failure before it began. They lived the life, luring their victims through the door, spinning a web of deceit so strong the victims remained trapped until the black widow and her partner fleeced them for every crumb that they possessed. Only then did they set them free, with nothing to call their own.

No one could stop them. Disappearing into the night when anyone got too close. They partied hard for days on end, fuelled by drugs and a hate for each other and the world. Plotting and planning and searching for the next victim to lure into their web of lies. He gambled their ill-gotten wealth away as fast as she dragged it in.

The black widow began to plot. She had found an unlikely partner. One she could use but not one she could trust. They were living the high life, on stolen wealth. But his greed and gambling were beginning to make life hard. She had to work harder than she wanted, to lure her victims in and spin a web of deceit. The life she had planned, a frivolous one with an endless supply of cash was slowly being eroded away. Many of those she mixed with were beginning to doubt the sincerity with which she tried to sell her schemes. It would soon be time to part ways, that she knew. How was the question. She needed to find a way without him trapping her and sending them both spinning down the road to ruin.

She spied the young couple, at one of her sales pitch presentations. They seemed so young and in love she couldn't resist. It should be an easy task to lure them into her web, with false promises and hope. They needed money to start their own life and she was happy to oblige. But she knew she wasn't on her usual game. Her underling was worrying her with his foolhardy spending of all their accumulated wealth. It was a distraction she didn't need.

The signs were all there, the couple oh-ed and ah-ed as she handed them the glossy brochures. The real estates were in a pristine location with an ocean view. The perfect investment. Little cash was needed up front. A group scheme where investors bought the land as a consortium. *With the cash you rake in you will soon have your own piece of paradise.* She had them caught on a fine thread of silk. One built on lies. Before her greedy eyes, she could see the cash rolling in.

They signed on the dotted line, promising to return within the week with their documents of proof to show they could meet their obligations, and with access to their bank accounts, or so she hoped.

By the week's end as promised, they returned to the office she rented just for show. She opened the door and showed them in. The spider waiting to lure them into her web. They bought with them a surprise she didn't expect. They were not alone. Outside the window she saw the cars, blue lights flashing and soon her parlour was filled with the men in blue.

Her web was destroyed, the spider was trapped.

One did escape though. Her partner in crime was nowhere to be found.

One Morning
Garry Davies

One morning, the sun came up in the usual place and the giant looked out his window.

'Boing!' something said. And then, 'Boing!' again.

'It's Spring,' said the giant. He went outside. The sky was clear and blue, and the air was cool and fresh.

'Boing!' said Spring, in a fresh, new and uncertain sort of voice.

The next morning, the sun came up and the giant looked out his window.

'Hello!' something said, and then, 'Hello!' again.
The giant went outside. Something was falling on his head. He went inside and fetched his umbrella.

'Hello!' something said when he was outside again.

'It's Hail,' said the giant.

'Hello!' called Hail, in a crisp and chilly voice.

The next morning when the giant woke up the sun came up in its usual place. The giant looked out the window and saw that it was dull and cloudy.

'Ouch!' something said. And then, 'Ouch!' again.

The giant, who by now had got up more than once in his life, immediately went into his shed. He came out with his rake.

'Ouch!' something said again, in a thin and brittle voice.

'It's Fall,' said the giant, and he began to rake up the leaves.

Outback Escape
Tania Park

Their peace had been shattered.

Beth wriggled her feet into well-worn but comfortable boots, careful not to spill a drop of wine; red this time because to chill the white in the tiny caravan fridge was difficult when they needed every square millimetre for food. The ice in the Esky had melted days ago.

Red dust settled on top of her boots at every step. Rain had been scant for a so long, the land had been left in myriad shades of brown and the top layers nothing but dense fine dust.

The almost full moon and welcome flicker of flames in the large circle of stones, made it easy to track to the log where she settled her backside. The seat is far enough from the fire to keep her warm but not so close she will bake. It is also upwind from the smoke and the same place she sat last night when there had only been the two of them but two more vans pulled in not long ago. A sigh escaped as she leant back against a tree-trunk, her flesh filling the rough voids in the bark. Somehow, the prickle was comforting. It was the solitude in these remote areas she enjoyed the most - the escape from reality: the reason they stayed more than a night. Now she was sorry they hadn't moved on.

'Hi, mind if I join you?'

Regret surged as Beth studied the owner of the voice. Well-worn rubber thongs flicked dust up sun-browned legs. Stubbie shorts were so creased it appeared they were welded to the man's hips. A faded navy singlet exposed a hairy chest and weather-beaten but well-muscled arms. The clean-shaven face was an anomaly as was the pleasant scent of citrus as the man neared.

'Feel free,' said Beth, waving one hand to indicate the circle around the fire.

The man unfurled an aluminium picnic chair, wriggled it in the dirt to ensure it was stable before he settled on the nylon webbing with a creak.

'Name's Johnno, where are you headed?' He clicked open a beer can. Yeast joined citrus the very second Johnno yanked the tab from the can and pocketed it.

'I'm Beth; headed north to no-where in particular. You? Where are you headed?'

'Towards a flock of three thousand dusty wethers in need of a haircut. My crew's already there doing the muster.'

'You the boss man?'

Johnno laughed. 'Technically but don't tell my wife. She likes to think she's the boss.'

'Is she with you?'

'Sally is already with the gang, probably issuing orders and making demands on the station owner. I had to settle the young'uns in boarding school after their holidays.'

Both turned their heads at the bang of a door. Two people emerged from an ancient campervan parked on the far side of the overnight camp stop. Young, Beth guessed but it was hard to tell from a distance. The guy picked up two folded stools and an Esky while the woman tagged behind. There was something in her hand but Beth couldn't make it out until the couple neared and revealed a plastic bowl.

Very young, Beth decided and shook her head. Had to be teenagers. The lad dropped the Esky, flicked each stool open and plonked them down. Puffballs of dust rose, scattered and fell. He sat, dragged the Esky over with his foot and lifted the lid. Fear lived in the girl's eyes as she eased down onto the other stool and huddled against her partner's side with a tight grip on his elbow. The girl's demeanour sent a wave of unease across Beth's shoulders.

'Hi, I'm Beth. This is Johnno and my husband, Dan, will be out soon. He's getting cleaned up.' Beth forced a laugh. 'Takes a bit longer when there aren't any ablution blocks. Shaving's a pain, he reckons.'

'Tony and this is Emma.'

'Where are you headed?' Johnno asked.

The girl winced as the couple glanced at each other. The glance said a lot. The wince told a deeper story.

'North. Plenty of work up north, after this Covid hoo-ha that prevented backpackers from coming,' said Tony. Instant relief washed over Emma's face.

'You got jobs lined up?' asked Beth.

'Nah, not yet but we made enquiries and most hospitality places are screaming for workers. Em's got her barista certificate and I can do about anything. Done the serving alcohol course. Got the paper to say I'm a responsible adult and can work in licenced premises.'

Beth bet he had only just qualified for he must barely be eighteen although some people looked much younger than they really were. Pity she wasn't one of them. At the moment she felt every minute of her age after the gruelling past few months.

'Hi'ya, all.' Dan waved a hand in greeting as he sat next to Beth and placed his plastic wine glass at his feet. 'You okay?' he whispered to Beth.

'Yes, I'm fine.' She took a sip of wine, appreciated the depth of flavour as another round of introductions were made. She'd lied but Dan knew she had. Fine had not been a part of their vocabulary since the accident. A wash of tears made everything hazy. She fought them away and forced her mind to concentrate on the people around her. Johnno, the clean-cut shearer who took the time to ensure his kids were settled in school, and with a wife who worked with him. She bet the couple hadn't worked during the school holidays but had ensured they spent quality time as a family. She also bet their family hadn't been torn apart by a drugged up hooligan who thought it was fun to hoon around the streets while high as a kite on alcohol and ice. Beth sniffed back the threatening tears. Dan slid his arm around her shoulders, tugged her closer. He knew she still struggled, the same way she knew he did, in his own way. They'd both shed oceans of tears, together and in private.

A pleasant silence settled over the little group, broken by constant cicada chirrups, the snap of burning wood, and the occasional scuffle of nightlife hidden out there in the dark beyond the shadows. Everyone stared into the flames and took the occasional sip of their beverages. The young girl drank cola - another clue to her age. Emma popped the lid from the plastic bowl and handed it around. At least she had manners and wasn't selfish. Everyone took a couple of crisps and crunched before washing the remnants down. Salty residue was strong but pleasant.

Beth allowed herself to be mesmerised by the flames, trying to make out shapes in the flickers, savouring the aroma of burning eucalyptus. Anything to free her mind of memories.

A flash of lights and crunch of tyres jarred the atmosphere. Emma shrank behind Tony's back. Johnno released a long whistle at the sight of the huge motorhome.

Emma straightened; her shoulders heaved in relief.

The motorhome came to a standstill slap bang in the middle of the gravel site, within touching distance of the other three vans. Just dandy. The owners couldn't possibly be discreet and park at a distance.

As he got out, they all stared at the driver. Grey haired, his clothes were pristine: moleskins, a studded western-style shirt and R.M Williams boots. Slack jaws joined the stares as they watched him take out a generator, plug it in to the electrical outlet and start the thing. It wasn't one of the new-fangled silent generators like Dan had bought. The inside of the motorhome lit up so bright it would be seen from space. The noise was an infringement of human rights.

Beth shook her head at the sight of the woman who emerged from the door. Blonde curls on the sixty something head had to be bleached. Tight skin on the heavily made-up face made it obvious the woman kept a plastic surgeon in a high life. The body, barely covered by tight, skimpy shorts and a sleeveless cotton blouse, was beyond skinny. The clothes revealed flabby wrinkles which should never be exposed to anyone other than the owner. Bright red toenails peeked from white high-heeled sandals. High heels? Out in the back of beyond? And white?

The man set up a padded fold-up chair and the woman perched on the front. 'Hi,' she said in such a way Beth knew it wasn't a word in the woman's normal vocabulary.

A similar chair unfolded next to Blondie. Out came a tray on which stood two tall crystal glasses and a bottle of champagne glistening with moisture. The man sat, popped the cork and filled the two glasses with the frothing liquid. Droplets of condensation reflected the orange flames like jewels.

'You have to be kidding me.' Beth twisted her head towards the whispered words from Johnno.

She smirked at Johnno's raised eyebrows. Dan nudged her and snorted under his breath. You see and meet all sorts out in the bush but this couple was at the top of the ladder in ridiculousness.

'Jackson Phillips,' said the man as he pointed to his own chest. 'My wife, Priscilla.' His hand wavered in front of the woman as he smiled. Priscilla gave a sort of smile but little on the face had the ability to move.

A muffled pig grunt came from Johnno as he tried to stifle his laughter. Beth had to look away to hide her grin. The names suited the couple so well.

'Nice rig,' said Dan.

'Thank you, it's new. Our first journey. Just retired,' said Jackson.

'What's with the generator?' asked Johnno. 'Surely you have separate batteries for overnight stays.'

'Yes, but…' began Jackson.

'We can't waste them,' butted in his wife.

Johnno lost it with a guffaw of laughter. Dan stood and disappeared into the darkness. Beth bit the inside of her cheek while she watched Emma's eyes widen and her mouth form a perfect circle. The grin on Tony's face almost split it in half.

For the next half hour precious Priscilla regaled them with name-dropping about the life of the obscenely rich. She even revealed to the last dollar, how much the motorhome had cost. No-one else said a thing. Beth didn't need to wonder why.

Johnno was the first to head for his small off-road van with a wave of his hand as he said good night. Beth headed for the bush to find a hidden dark spot to relieve her bladder, and almost jumped out of her skin when footsteps thudded behind.

'Can I come with you?' asked Emma. 'I'm scared of the dark.'

Beth paused. 'Sure thing but find another bush.' They walked side-by side for about thirty metres. Beth pointed. 'There's a good bush. You go there. I'll go over here.' She indicated a bush in the opposite direction.

'Please wait for me?' There was a definite quiver of fear in the plea.

Two minutes later they met in the same spot. 'What are you running from?' Beth dared ask.

Fear shot across Emma's face. 'What makes you think I'm running?'

'It's obvious but I can keep a secret. Are you okay?'

'I am now. Tony is my brother.'

'Your brother?' It was the last thing Beth expected to hear. 'You're not in a relationship with your brother are you?'

'Eww, no, of course not.' Emma shivered. 'He got me away.'

'Away from what?'

'My stepfather. He's…' she sniffed. 'Evil. Ever since Mum died. He gets drunk, yells… hits me… sneaks into my room at night.'

'He sexually assaulted you?' Beth grasped the girl around the shoulders to prevent her walking any further.

'No, not yet, but he peeks through the keyhole, barges into my bedroom when he thinks I'm getting undressed. See this?' Even in the semi-dark a whopping bruise with yellowed edges emerged as she lifted the bottom of her T-shirt. 'I told Tony every time the bastard hit me. We made plans. Saved up as much as we could from our jobs. I stole some from the pig, emptied my account. We bought the old camper and hid it at a friend's place. I turned eighteen three days ago. Tony is twenty. Now I am an adult the bastard can't stop me or call the cops on me. We're going as far north as we can. We'll work and save then move interstate to start over.'

A wodge of emotion jammed in Beth's throat. 'I'm sorry you have to do that.' Beth wrapped the girl up in her arms, hugged her tight. 'You sound like you're a tough cookie. Before you leave in the morning I'll give you my contact details. If you ever need any help, you call me. We're also going north for a few months so maybe we won't be far away.' She kept one arm around Emma's shoulders as they walked back to camp. 'I lost my daughter a few months back. Car accident. She was only sixteen. So maybe you can help me at the same time by letting me be a substitute mum.' For the first time, a barbed spear didn't tear at her innards at the mention of her daughter.

'Oh, gosh, I'm sorry. Mum died from cancer six months ago. It tore me apart even though I knew it was terminal. I was glad when she died because she was in so much pain but it still hurts inside me all the time.'

Beth had to swipe the tears from her cheeks. 'It's never easy to lose someone you love. Dan and I came away on this trip to get out of the house – escape the emptiness. It's hard to explain but the outback seems to have healing powers.'

'I understand and thank you.'

'For what?' Beth asked as they stopped by the fire, now burnt down to gold embers and white ash. With no plant life within cooee and little breeze, there was no chance it would flare up and become dangerous.

'For caring. For understanding.'

'You are very welcome. Make sure you keep in touch and good night.'

'Night.'

Beth kept her eyes on the girl until she crawled into her van. Before going to her own van, she stalked over to the generator, threaded her fingers around the cord and yanked hard until silence reigned. To make sure, she bundled the cord up and threw it under the centre of the motorhome, doubtful either Mr or Mrs Moneybags would lower themselves to crawl underneath for fear of getting dirt on their pristine clothes.

Guilt for both her thoughts and actions, flared as she shot into her van and grinned at Dan who raised his eyebrows. 'Smart woman,' he said as they both undressed, climbed into bed and switched off the light, stifling their laughter at the shrill voices outside.

They actually laughed, she thought, as Dan spooned behind her and wrapped an arm around her middle.

An Email
To the Aunt Who Loved Me
(Florence Beatrice Sharp: 3rd Feb 1888 – 23rd Sep 1986)
Graham Chapman

Hi Auntie Flo,

Think I like, Dear Great Aunt Flo better. Now don't hit me with your wisdom stick!

It's been a while. I often think of you as you pop into my mind often, and especially when I write stories about the Sharps. Uncle Bruce and Aunty Joyce produced a great story about the Littlejohn's, and you get a really good mention there. Not big enough mind you but they had a lot of rellies to write about. There is a great photo of your mum and dad.

I'm the keeper of your mother's photo album. Ronis has most of your postcards and I have a small number. Two of your postcards were of great historical interest to the State Library. One Bob sent you, assume not Uncle Rob, with a photo of Subiaco and the other, the Meekatharra one, of you, Grandma, Ettie and John Fisher's wife and sister-in-law. It's also in the Meekatharra library and I wrote a story about it.

I often think about you and Grandma in Meeka, so far from home in the desert and working as dressmaker and piano teacher. I found your ads in the local paper.

Do you remember Sunday drives in Pa's car. And how slow he drove during the day that year we came home from Canberra. Anyhow, one Saturday night some years ago, I remembered driving through middle park and that you said, "We used to live up there". I took it in somehow. Anyhow, this Saturday evening I remembered this vividly and the road, cause it's a prominent one, off Beaconsfield Parade. So, I started looking it up. We don't need street directories anymore. I'll explain that another time, although I have an old Melbourne one still. Worked out it was Kerferd Road and checked out old electoral rolls and death certificates about your mother and father. We can do this on a computer these days. I'll explain that another time as well.

I now have some idea of how significant the place was. Your mother died there, about the same age as my mum died. Your dad moved there because the 1890s bust had knocked him around financially. Uncle Bruce says he was a newsagent. Quite a change from a builder speculator. I also remember sitting with you as we drove along maybe Punt Road and you talked about how something was the Sharp buildings. I've not worked out where that was, but what I realise more and more you were telling me about significant times in your life. You were thirteen, and Grandma nine when your mum died at a time of great financial turmoil for your father. Your little stories to me have become more powerful over the years. Thank you. I was lucky to have you. I loved putting my finger in front of your face as we sat in lounge room at 53 and you'd laugh and giggle. Usually, you'd say, 'Stop it Bruce'. I never got upset when you called me Bruce. I realise how much you loved him and me. I told him about this a few years before he died.

Better go, getting quite emotional writing to you.

Love Graham.

P.S. Swans were good last week. They win finals & premierships these days.
P.P.S. I've stood outside where you lived in Prahran, Brunswick & Kerferd Rd.

Generations
Nicole Corsini

Waves crash along the coast as far as the eye can see, travelling up onto the land until it disappears, soaked up by the smooth beige sand. The sun shines but the air is cold. The lady is glad she decided at the last minute to chuck on jeans and her favourite dark red, knitted jumper which had been a birthday gift from her Mum.

She picks a spot to sit on the large black rocks, which somewhat resembled giant pieces of charcoal taking up more territory than the sand. Leaning back, she supports herself by placing linked hands around her knee bent up towards her chest.

With closed eyes she takes a long exaggerated breath, consciously trying to make the muscles in her body relax on the exhale. The shoulders fall slowly as she releases the tension being held within. Another deep breath, shoulders fall further. One more breath, but the limit has been reached of what she can let go of for now.

Slowly she opens her eyes and is brought right back to the beach. Her mind playing over the morning and the fight she had with her daughter - again. Mad at herself for not remaining calm as she keeps promising she will, mad at her daughter for being so selfish and mad that nothing is changing.

It was supposed to be different with her daughter. She was always going to be the person she wanted her Mum to be when she was fourteen, but she's not. Often quick to anger, constantly stressed, forever overwhelmed. Rarely laughing and only on occasions having fun. She was just like her mother.

Overcome with the familiar feeling of regret and guilt, she wanted to see her daughter, to hold her and say, 'everything will be okay.' There were still five hours until school would be finished so first, she would make a stop on the way to see the woman who raised her, her Mum. The Mum who was once quick to anger, constantly stressed, forever overwhelmed. Who had rarely laughed and only on occasions had fun. The Mum she knew would now hug her and tell her, 'This time is hard, but I promise everything will be okay.'

She stretches one leg down in front of the rock until her foot meets the sand, then repeats with the other leg. She stands, stretches her arms high into the air, soaks in a few more seconds of the view. One more deep breath, she inhales strength from the sea, turns and starts to walk up the beach, back to her life. Hopeful it would be different this time.

A Dangerous Mission
Dot Wilson

Jean-Claude could run no longer. He flattened himself against the wall of the tunnel and listened intently for any sound of the enemy, a task made more difficult by the thumping sound of his own heart resounding in his sizeable ears. His skin prickled in the muggy warmth, made just bearable by the kilometres of pipeline with cooling water pumped through them to control the heat. The eerie glow of the fairly basic lighting only added to his discomfort and enhanced his sense of being in a hostile landscape, although in reality it was the only home he had ever known.

Finally, satisfied they had given up the pursuit, he adjusted his beret to a rakish angle, gave his whiskers a little twirl, and finally smoothed down the sparse hairs on his long pink tail.

'*Sacre bleu*, that was close,' he muttered as he jogged slowly but steadily towards the rendezvous point, symbolically almost exactly halfway along the length of the Channel Tunnel, to meet up with other members of the underground resistance from the countries at either end.

They were all there, anxiously waiting for him: the small band of English mice, led by the battle-scarred. Pete, and the delectable, Doris, who wore a tiny dagger tucked into a belt at her waist. Jean-Claude deliberately avoided her adoring gaze - the life of a renegade rodent tended to be short and he would not allow himself to become attached to anyone.

'Jean-Claude my friend, at last. You had us worried,' cried Pete, relief audible in his voice.

'I had a run in with that damned ginger tom, I only just escaped,' replied Jean-Claude, 'I will be more careful next time. It is good to see you, *mon ami*, it has been too long. As we are all here, let us put our heads together and come up with a plan to deal with these tunnel cats who seek to make our lives miserable.'

'My sources in the Tunnel Authority offices have advised me there are plans to trap the cats, so the problem may be taken care of soon, but they are notoriously difficult to catch, so I think we need to do something to assist the trappers. Does anyone have any ideas?' asked Pete.

That started a noisy exchange of opinions which went on for some time, occasionally becoming very heated. There was a break for refreshments, with a pleasant surprise of some tasty morsels acquired from the lunch leftovers of a French work detail who had been doing some repairs on the railway tracks. Good bread and excellent cheese was a rare treat and kept morale high.

Finally, after a few hours of brainstorming and argument, interrupted a couple of times by the roar of a train rushing past, the intrepid warriors had come up with a plan. They parted ways with many a slap on the back, agreeing to meet again to put their plan into place when word came through from their contacts in the Tunnel Authority that the cat trapping was about to commence.

Three weeks later, a message was received. The trapping would begin in three days' time. Final arrangements were made, with a relay system of couriers passing on the last details of the plan from one end of the tunnel to the other. At last, the day arrived, and all the mice gathered at the meeting point not far from where the trapping was about to take place. They could hear the trappers talking and the clank of metal traps being removed from vehicles and put into place. The traps were made of wire mesh, and food placed inside to tempt the cat to enter. If the cat went in far enough, its weight pressed down on a metal plate which triggered the release of the door that had been held open at one end, and hey presto, one trapped and usually very angry cat. The problem was, the feral cats were very wily and very cautious and often would not put a paw inside the trap, no matter how hungry they were.

The band of intrepid resistance fighters kept hidden as they heard the work crew packing up and the vehicles drive off back to their base. Two lookouts were posted to watch for any hungry feline that might try to catch them unawares. Then they swung into action, moving in pairs to each trap to take up position and wait. Jean-Claude and Pete were together. They made their way to the furthest capture site, took up position close to the trap, behind a cooling pipe. They settled down to wait, talking very softly, with their ears pricked for the slightest sound. The wait wasn't long.

The ginger tom crept slowly into view, tail twitching nervously as he approached the cage. It was the first chance Jean-Claude had had to get a close look at his adversary for he was usually too busy running hell for leather in the opposite direction. The enormous feline was missing one eye, and both ears were somewhat shredded looking. The old warrior had obviously had some close encounters throughout his hard life. He stood at the entrance to the cage, whiskers quivering as he sniffed the air, savouring the smell of the tasty bowl of cat food beckoning to him from the other end of the trap. The two mice held their breath when the old tom raised one paw as if to step into the trap. But he hesitated, then backed slowly off and began to walk away.

This was the cue for the two mice; they swung into action. Jean-Claude had drawn the short straw. He ran out into the open in front of the entrance to the trap. Pete hid close by; if the unthinkable should happen and Jean-Claude was caught, the fight must go on. Pete would take JeanClaude's place to lure the tomcat into the cage.

Jean-Claude gave a little squeak. It was enough to catch the cat's attention. He was about a metre in front of the entrance, as the cat, slowly at first, crept towards him, belly flat on the ground, eyes fixed on his prey, the tip of his tail twitching in jerks. Jean-Claude held his ground - until he judged the time to be right. He turned and dashed for the cage. As soon as he took off, the cat accelerated behind him, closing the distance between them at an alarming rate.

Pete drew in a sharp breath as he watched his friend be hunted, unable to even shout encouragement lest he distract the tom from his purpose. The little French mouse dashed into the cage and straight over the trigger plate, his weight nowhere near enough to set it off. The tom cat, now with only the thought of catching his prey on his mind, was closing the gap. He stretched out a paw to swipe the little rodent but Jean-Claude had timed it perfectly and dashed out through the mesh of the cage to safety, while the cat's weight on the plate triggered the release mechanism and the door slammed down with a satisfying snap. The old ginger tom hissed and spat, but to no avail; he was well and truly caught.

The two friends clasped each other in their paws and did a little victory dance. Together they eyed their long-time adversary with satisfaction, then turned on their heels and headed for the meeting place. There, they met up with their comrades-in-arms and learned that all but one of their compatriots had returned safe. Sadly, one of the French mice had stumbled and fallen prey to the cat coming close behind her. Several of the cats had entered the traps by themselves and the teams had not had to place themselves in danger. The mice acknowledged their victory with a small celebration, including a heartfelt toast to their fallen comrade. The underground rebels had won the day, and secured a safer existence for themselves, for a while at least. They said their farewells and made their separate ways home for a well-deserved rest, and to reflect on their victory and the peace it would bring them.

Jean-Claude scrambled up a thick electrical cable and paused at the top. He glanced back at the band of his English comrades-in-arms as they steadily made their way back home. He saw Doris, her tiny shapely figure silhouetted for a second against a light when she stopped and turned to look in his direction, head held high. Today had given Jean-Claude some cause for reflection. Yes, life could be cut unfairly short, but perhaps that was the best reason of all to take a chance and experience all that it had to offer, including a chance at love. Smiling quietly to himself, he turned for home, already planning the next joint venture with his northern friends.

The Welcome
Dianne Morton

A town with no electricity, no cars, no shops, cut off from the world outside. Empty houses waiting for something or someone. A little town anywhere in outback Australia.

Six misfits boarded a bus to an outback town. They didn't know where they were going. Looking for adventure or escaping from life, it didn't matter, as none of it mattered.

The priest, Paul, (Minister, Father, Brother, Man of the Cloth, Man of God) or whatever, for none of it mattered, as none of the above was true. He waited patiently for his flock to arrive, then watched as they staggered from the bus onto the road. It's cracked and worn surface told a tale of neglect. The bus departed, returning from whence it came.

He had asked for and received a flock to help rebuild this town so the congregation could call this place home. Being a Man of God or whatever, for none of it was true, he took in whoever came his way. He willingly accepted anyone who came forward. He didn't discriminate for all were equal.

He studied his list and the motley crew who stood before him. Eight hardy souls of God (*he hoped*) and six chickens as an extra side. He welcomed the couple first. They were one, he didn't know which one and none of it mattered. He needed a couple to settle the rest, but he wasn't sure they were up to the task.

Next on his list was the elderly lady. He had chosen her, for a flock always needs one of experience and a guiding hand. Mrs Murphy, the lady in question, leaned heavily on her stick and scowled at Cleo and Leo. Of what use she would be, was still to be determined.

A plumber, he needed a plumber for the town had water tanks to bring the water in and septic tanks to take it out. One stood before him. 'Plumber by name,' he said, 'not by trade, but he did know,' he said, 'that water tanks bring the water in, and the septic tanks take the water out.' He didn't sound very reliable, but the priest, Paul, took what he was given, and none of it mattered, for he needed help.

Father Paul, or whatever, for none of it was true, shook his head where a single tuft of hair flicked back and forth, for that was all he had. He questioned Sparky, who had the word electrician in brackets after his name. 'Was he indeed an electrician by trade?'

Sparky's eyes lit up and he nodded his head in agreement. His body had not a spare bit of skin that wasn't covered in tattoos or body piercings. His long-matted hair covered his eyes, but none of that mattered, for all were welcome.

Brother Paul, or whatever, for none of it was true, hoped they had sent a handyman to fix the things that needed fixing. Hopefully one of his flock could do the tasks required.

She stood before him, an apparition maybe, for a thing of slender beauty she was. A handyman she was not.

'A handywoman I am,' she told him. Her blonde hair shook, and the long eyelashes blinked at him. 'I am here to wait for the congregation as I thought I might serve them. They might have need of a little comfort.'

How to respond he had no idea for he wondered what type of comfort she meant to offer.

The last and maybe the least of his flock leaned against a wall of one of the buildings. He wasn't on the list, but he welcomed all who came. Bruce by name, he was told. Bruce, a big and rotund man offered no knowledge or help. He came to watch, for a flock needed watching. He would just watch if that was okay.

The poor priest Paul, or whatever, for none of it was true, threw up his hands in despair. He told his rabble to go and find a house to call their own and start making this town a place for the congregation to live. He retreated to his belfry and prayed to whoever might be listening. He needed a miracle to bring his flock together and make the town a place to live. Intervention was what he sought.

Now the couple, Cleo and Leo, chose the first house they came across. Sparky made to leave to find a house next to theirs, but Mrs Murphy she did growl. Sparky snatched up the crate of chickens and bolted from the scene.

Bruce just stood and watched, for that is what he had come to do. Handywoman made for the house on the far edge of town. She would wait until the congregation arrived.

That left Plumber by name, not trade, to find a house, and one look from Mrs Murphy, who had chosen the house next to the couple, made him wish he didn't have to stay. Left with little choice, he found a house next to Handywoman.

Young Sparky, with a grin on his face from ear to ear, soon had the old generator rattling to life. He was covered in tattoos and now he was covered in grease. An electrician or a mechanic was still unclear and yet to be determined.

Cleo and Leo came out of their house, they needed lights that didn't dance a merry jig on the ceiling. They wanted Sparky to solve the problem, but Sparky just shook his head.

Mrs Murphy appeared from nowhere. She looked askance at Sparky, who shook all over. Cleo and Leo looked down at their polished nails.

Mrs Murphy, she banged her stick on the ground, growled, and snarled like a rabid dog at Cleo and Leo, who beat a hasty retreat. Sparky bolted from the scene.

Plumber by name, not by trade, came by. Mrs Murphy, she changed in an instance and with a charming smile invited him in. She needed fresh water from the tank to come in, not the septic. Plumber he might not be, but he was happy to help an old lady in need.

Now this bunch of misfits settled in and slowly the town started to come to life. Minister Paul or whatever, for none of it mattered, as none of the above was true, nodded his head. He was surprised and spent a lot of time in his belfry thanking whoever might be listening, then praying that none of his flock would come to harm.

A bunch of misfits was his flock, but they had found their place. Cleo and Leo were seen banging a nail or two in here or pulling a weed or two there. Sparky kept the generator going and the lights dancing a merry jig on the ceiling. He talked to the six chickens, who gave him some golden eggs. Bruce, he did what he did best, just watched, but he did produce a vegetable patch that was the pride of the town.

Mrs Murphy, continued to scare Cleo and Leo, snarling and growling, whenever they came near. As for Handywoman, none of the flock knew what she did, that was still to be determined.

Father Paul or whatever, for none of it mattered, as none of the above was true, did the best he could to guide his flock, which was very little, save for a prayer or two.

Entry to Paradise
Janusz Zejdler

At the end of the Second World War in 1945, there were many thousands of refugees, former slave workers, captured by the nazis, who were homeless and needed care. Not all could return to their country of birth, they had to be expatriated to one of the many free countries which offered to take them in. One of many teenagers, Stefan, whose parents lost their lives during their enslaved work, was provided with such an opportunity. He was one month short of his 16th birthday, still he met the sixteen-year-old criteria and chose to live in Australia.

Stefan boarded a Panama ship, SS FAIRSEA, in Naples, Italy. It was a modified troop carrier during the war and now had an Italian captain and crew. The ocean welcomed the passengers with a rocking motion which was comfort for some but not others. Stefan turned out to be a very good sailor. They passed through the Suez Canal, created by the manual efforts of thousands of human beings. Its banks held buildings, families, and hotels. The hotel clients came outside, lifting their long white shirts and waving their private parts in greeting. The trip was a learning experience for Stefan, who not only suffered rejection from the strange and foreign world they steamed past, but also experienced at first hand the ocean liner, how it worked inside and out, and the ocean life day and night.

The weather became warmer. Passengers chose to sleep on deck. It brought some concerns for the captain, of possible overreaching friendship between the passengers and crew. The captain soon stopped this by keeping his crew in a restricted part of the ship and the passengers in another.

The three weeks of sailing were pure joy for Stefan, experiencing something new and satisfying each hour he spent on deck or below it in the engine room. Nearing the coast of Australia, the days began earlier, and the nights were shorter. He would stand by the rails and look over the ocean, trying to make some sense of the volume of water across the whole of his vision in all directions. But the most unexplained occurrence to this day was the dolphins appearing out of nowhere and swimming either along the ship or in front of it, maintaining their distance without any effort or evident movement of any part of their bodies. During the evening, the flying fish would appear, some with lights on.

A cyclone warning was given about a week away from the destination, and the captain set a course around it with only some swelling of the seas, which was an experience. Being on deck and watching the storm from right or left, the ship moving from side-to-side, creating the visual effect of the sea or the sky only. Many people went below to avoid nature's exhibition of its power and, at the same time, its creativity and beauty, even during not-so-calm performances.

It was three weeks since departing Napoli. SS FAIRSEA navigates the Mediterranean Sea through the Suez Canal and the Red Sea into the Gulf of Aden, the Arabian Sea, and the Indian Ocean. She neared the destination of Western Australia. On that morning, as if on cue, all rushed to the top deck to secure the best position to look towards where land was expected to appear. When they were close enough to see individual structures in the new home, some newcomers did not do well. The buildings were constructed of corrugated iron and not brick. This created concerns about the country's promised wealth and the newcomers' future well-being. Despite these concerns, when the time came to disembark, all went smoothly until more creative passengers brought more of the allowed duty-free cigarettes and had to hand them over. Those still on deck, seeing what was taking place, looked through their hand luggage, checked their goodies, and distributed them among the rest of the family. One creative lady with slightly more than a slim figure and a long loose dress had tied a few cartons of cigarettes around her waist and strung them down her body. Unfortunately, the Custom Officers noticed, and her creativity was spoiled.

Stefan boarded the steam-operated train from Fremantle to the next destination over sixty miles away, Northam. Stopping at Perth Station and onto the Midland Junction track was just as exciting as that from Fremantle to Perth. After the initial shock of seeing Fremantle Port, this section restored the newcomer's expectations that Australia was a progressive and modern country. It is essential to mention that 1950 had a hot summer. There was a burn-off to reduce the risk of bushfire. When the train reached half-way up Greenmount hill, with the fire and smoke around the train, there was much crying, almost screaming, not knowing what was happening. Considering what some of those on the train have experienced in concentration camps, they thought they were being taken to something similar. Given an offer to return to Europe at this moment, most would likely have taken it. Who in their right mind sets a fire in hot weather?

At the Northam camp, Stefan waited for a more permanent place to stay. The weather was hot, and following the long journey, he was thirsty and looked for a tap where water was found. He found the tap, which had some writing on it, he didn't understand. The one word he understood was 'water.' This was good enough for him, so he had a drink, and, in return, got a mouth full of dam water. Later, he found the sign on the tap read 'Dam Water-Unfit for Drinking.'

There were no English classes for the residents and only some schooling for the young. Teenagers could not benefit from any of the academic services. Math levels were comparable, but not the language. Stefan had the experience of attending one class, and during question time, he asked what he thought was a very brave and clever demonstration of his English. He asked the lady teacher (a retired primary school teacher), 'How old are you?' and was quickly put in place by her reply.

'It is rude in this country to ask a lady her age. But seeing as you asked me, I will tell you, I am older than my teeth but younger than my tongue.' And that was the end of the English class.

The camp offered many activities, including Scouts and Girl Guides. One event that Stefan recollects and feels guilty about to this day, was during the Easter season. Easter Friday is strictly observed in the Catholic religion by personal denial from any social celebrations. Unfortunately, the town's Anglican Church Girl Guides invited the Camp's Boy Scouts to an evening social with dancing, cakes, cool drinks and many other goodies and piano music for dancing to. That is where it all went wrong because of cultural ignorance and respect for each other. They participated in the refreshments but not the dancing, not that they didn't want to, but observing the religious obligations was essential. In addition to this problem, there was a communication barrier to explain. All the girl guides, following each other in line, came up to each of the boys and very courteously, with a smile, asked them to dance. The boys all felt bad in having to give their denial, but the girls felt much worse than they did.

Midland Junction Railway Workshops, with over 4,000 employees in every trade possible, called for an apprenticeship intake. It was sixty miles from the camp at Northam. Stefan applied with the support of the Camp Director, with whom he worked and who had his character reference. He was accepted for an interview. This meant attending the Midland Junction workshop and becoming a junior worker until selection time. Stefan was given the task of making lead seals. The wage was six pounds per fortnight. There was no set target for the daily production, but learning the work culture was soon discovered to be essential. One day, Stefan made what he thought was a reasonable effort. But one of the old-timers came up and spoke.

'Listen, Sonny, someone on light duties or sick normally does this job, so keep it modest.'

So, he did. But the assistant supervisor came up in the next few days and spoke.

'What happened? You are not as productive as you were a few days ago. Are you sick? You better put some effort into it to keep your job.'

As time went on, Stefan rented a small house, and for that time (the early nineteen-fifties) there were 'modern' furniture and kitchen requirements. To keep food fresh, a Coolgardie Cooler was used with its block of ice, delivered each Thursday. A toilet pan was placed under the toilet seat and cleared each week and replaced with a cleaned, empty one. It wasn't until much later, in 1955, that technology caught up: a Kelvinator Fridge still working in 2023 and a sewerage system for the toilet. The Kelvinator fridge is in Stefan's shed to keep his beer cold.

As time marched on, so did Stefan. He had a few job changes and a single, reasonably active, life despite the shifts away from home. He worked almost around the clock and was on a call with just six hours' notice, day or night, during the week, weekends, or public holidays. At one point, on night duty, he complained to the foreman, who responded: 'My boy, if you haven't got a job you like, then like the job you got!'

Something Stefan took to heart and followed. It guided him well in achieving a solid future.

Working away from home meant sharing rooms with others, sometimes 3 to 5 in one room. One of the lads always slept in, which upset the day's target. So, one morning, one of the blokes got up a bit earlier and noticed that the late one was still asleep, with his body partly uncovered. Quickly and quietly, some warm water was poured slowly under his private parts. A few moments later, there was a show as the sleeping angel awakened but would not get up and covered himself up to his chin. To this day, he is unsure if he did the act or if others pulled a dirty trick on him. In the end, all parted good friends.

Once, Stefan nearly lost his life by being impatient during his many trips to and from the Midland Workshops while crossing the double-line train tracks. Trains simultaneously moved independently in both directions; there were no crossing boom gates, only flashing lights in operation. He was stopped at the level-crossing in Guildford opposite the post office. The train to Midland had just cleared the down main line, and he was ready to ride across and was between the two lines when the train to Guildford came out of nowhere. Stefan only just stopped clear and was very close to the locomotive. He could smell the hot oil from the moving parts as some splashed on him. It was a lesson to remember.

The six months spent in the workshop were worth it. Stefan did well in the new country by reinforcing the new language, learning the culture, and getting the feel of what may be faced in future. The last he was heard of he was a retired man celebrating his 90th birthday.

An Unfiltered Tale
Su Watson

It ain't the first time I've been here. But what you gunna do? Things happen, and then people, being people, take one look at me and decide it's my fault. Well, not this time. O' course, while she gets to wait on the comfy chairs, with potted plants and tissues, sniffing about what a victim she is, I'm the wrong-un stuck here in limbo.

In *my* waiting room there's a plastic canteen chair, set behind a' ugly metal table, where I'm s'posed to sit like a naughty school kid waiting for the other shoe to drop. Waiting is the name of the game here. And I must be as uncomfortable as possible, so I can cogitate on me crimes—a grown-up version of the naughty step, if you like. Well, I don't like. So, I smile, and waving my middle finger at the tiny red eye, winking at me from the ceiling in the corner, I drag the chair away from the table.

I slouch crookedly, with an arm hooked over the back and me legs stretched out in front. At least if I fall asleep this time, I won't slide off and look like a dick. Time passes slowly. There's no sound—no talking, no footsteps, not even the tick of a clock. I could be on the moon, but for the faint whiff of vomit and bleach. I stare at the empty walls, eyelids drooping. The door opens just as I'm drifting off.

The copper entering is a woman, and a looker too. I pull the chair closer to the table and tip it forward on two legs. I rest me chin on me hands as she sits. Dunno what's below the table but what's above looks quite a handful. She slaps a heavy folder down and it narrowly misses me nose. The sound ricochets off the tabletop, which shudders violently on wobbly legs. I grab for me chair before it slips away, and I bang me chin against the table or bite me lip. When I look up at the cop's face, it's as cold and hard as the table.

'Mr Spicer, perhaps you'd like to tell me in your own words what happened today.'

'Cup of coffee, love?' I say. 'I've been here hours. It's the least you can do.' I slouch backward again, rearranging the crown jewels which are now thrust toward her.

'I hear it was coffee that got you here in the first place, so we'll pass on that for now.' She shows not the slightest interest in me crown jewels, but it's not this that nettles me.

'Has she got a cup of coffee?' I ask. 'I'll bet she's got a cup, ain't she?' Me voice has grown loud and agitated.

'Mr Spicer, Jim. This will go better for both of us if we don't shout at one another. I am not here to talk about the other person. I'm here to find out from you what happened. So, let's start again, shall we? You were having a coffee with your dad, this morning, outside the Coffee Bean, yes?'

'Yeah,' I shuffle in me seat and look down at me hands. I wanna get this right. 'I go with the old boy every Tuesday. It's pension day see, so we have a bit of a catchup. Well, there we are, he's barely got his jam tart in his mouth when this bird sits down at the table opposite and gets her tits out.' I pause here and look up to see if the cop's as shocked by this as we were. But she's being professional, and I see she can't show no emotion, so I continue.

'Now me, I'm not averse to a free ogle if it's offered— though if you're asking, they were too big for my taste. Anyway, I'm sharin' this observation with the old boy and when I turn to look at him, he's turned a funny shade of red and he don't know where to put his face. So, I give him a nudge coz, you know, it's probably been a while for him since he's had a free show, and before we know what's happening, Miss Titsout is ranting and raving, and carrying on. She's yelling about how we're eating coz we're hungry, and her baby should be able to eat when it's hungry too, and she can do what she's doing without two dirty old men staring and talking about her tits. Well, the poor ole boy is choking by now, and I'm frightened he's gunna have a heart attack. So, I leap up and ask the waitress for some water. I'm slapping the poor old fella on the back, and he's coughing and gasping, and Titifa is still going. How it serves him right, and she hopes he dies, being as she shouldn't have to feed her baby in the toilet coz one stupid old man is embarrassed, and breastfeeding is a normal, natural bodily function. This last bit she yells really loud, just in case there's no-one left in the café what ain't seen or heard her making a spectacle of herself.

'Then I'm so mad, so mad that it's all about her, and what's right for her—and she's not even caring about my poor old dad, who is dying from embarrassment and choking, that I go over, drop me dacks, and shit on the pavement right next to her. And, it was a good effort, if I say so meself… But then she starts screaming like I'm murdering the baby, and someone's yelling how no-one wants to see that, and someone's calling the police, and then everyone's crowding round her like they think I really *am* going to murder the baby.'

So, I say, 'I don't know what your problem is. Shitting is a normal, natural bodily function.'

A Gothic Tale
Victoria Mizen

Okay, so you want Gothic. A dark and stormy night, a spooky castle with ugly, terrifying gargoyles, a cellar for imprisoning the gorgeous blonde damsel and of course a ghost or two as well as perhaps a witch.

Outside, wolves howl, lightning flashes, thunder roars, hurricane force winds belt through the trees and bash against the cobweb encrusted windows.

Inside, locked away in his library, which is situated on the ground floor, the old man sits behind the desk on which a solitary candle sputters, providing just enough light to accentuate shadows moving across the wall behind him. Curled up at his feet, Sabrina, his black cat, snuffles in her sleep.

Have I got the right atmosphere for you? But hang on, this is Australia. It's mid-summer, stinking hot, real hurricanes hanging around, ready to lash out at anyone stupid enough to not have battened down the hatches. The clock – that ancient model standing in the front hall, says it's nearly midnight. It, the clock, was carted here in 1856, on the good ship, 'Amrose,' along with all the other antiques that furnish this place.

This place, not exactly a castle, more like a huge country mansion, was built over the years 1857 – 1859, by convicts and aboriginals who were allocated to the master – Sir Cecil Billingsworth. The same Sir Cecil who carted his wife, two sons and a daughter, plus the furniture, paintings, silverware, porcelain, a grand piano and the clock, from his father's estate in Gloucestershire.

Like most of the landed gentry who arrived in Australia back then, he was allotted vast areas of land with access to the river, not too far from civilisation, where he was expected to produce food for the rapidly growing population in and around Sydney.

However, like most of the landed gentry, Sir Cecil had never actually got his hands dirty on the familial estate back in England. That's what the convicts and aborigines were for on his new estate and he knew how to treat them like the servants (paid or unpaid) that they were.

Some convicts, having arrived on previous ships, had earned their freedom and as they had worked very hard, on country estates back in England, they could rightfully claim fair treatment, decent wages, often accommodation, and sometimes a comely wife in return for their farming skills.

Jack Travis was one of those. Arriving at the Billingsworth's Australian landholding, he quickly sized up Sir Cecil, decided that lady Cecil was actually the brighter party, and soon had the whole family eating out of his hand. Well, not literally as his hands were often marked with mud and manure, but he did pretty much run the farm. And he did it well, only rarely pocketing a bit extra on the side for himself and the comely wench (formerly a very pretty convict lass.)

Back in England she was known for her sewing skills, so, once the house was built by the male convicts, under Jack's command, Mrs Travis made the clothes for Lady Cecil and her daughter and, when required, helped with acquiring materials for curtains, bedspreads and other decorative items. No-one bothered what she did with the leftovers.

Now, back to the Gothic bit. It's 1860, late January, hall clock about to strike midnight, tropical cyclone heading down the coast, rain pelting down causing the nearby river to overflow, lightening lighting up the black sky, thunder crashing loud enough to wake the dead, dingoes (sorry, no wolves here) slinking in the paddocks, huge trees that provide shade around the house, are swaying like ships at sea, threatening to smash the house down.

Next morning everyone awakes to devastation. The aborigines, peer out from their humpies which are situated at the far end of the home paddock, away from the threat of falling trees. Jack Travis, in his tiny mud cottage, is up with the sunrise. His wife is missing, but his first duty is to check on the animals in his care. He rouses the aborigines and the convicts, sending them off to repair fences, round up wounded or escaping cattle and sheep, clear fallen branches and trees, ensure they can all get to water and generally take care of farm jobs.

Assuming his wife is already at the big house, preparing breakfast for everyone, he takes two of his most reliable convicts and heads in that direction. Half way across the paddock, the men hear a scream from the master's study. Racing to the house is impossible, given the sodden state of the ground, but Jack and his assistants get there as quickly as they can.

Bessie, the convict housekeeper, greets them at the kitchen door. Her shaking hands and gaping mouth tell them that something is seriously amiss.

'Bessie, what's happened?' They all ask at once.

Without replying, she grabs Travis by the hand and staggers towards Sir Cecil's study. The master is slumped in his chair, blood now drying on the wound at the back of his head. A silver letter opener, dating from whenever such items were first used back in England, sits in its usual place on the desk.

His wife, traumatized by the sight of her murdered husband, weeps convulsively on the shoulder of her older son, Jonathon. The Billingsworth's younger son, Robert, better known to this lot as Bobby, is bawling his eyes out in the arms of his sister, Ursula.

Realising that one of the staff will be accused of this murder, Jack Travis takes charge. He beseeches Bessie to produce tea and, if she can calm herself, lashings of toast and jam. Everyone will need sustenance if they are to accomplish all the work ahead of them, inside and outside the house.

Harry, one of the convicts, almost ready for parole, is sent to fetch a horse and ride to Sydney. The police must be summoned.

Oliver, the other convict, best known for his ability to wheedle food out of those who have spares, heads off under instructions, to round up the best aboriginal trackers in the local mob and bring them to the house, along with Angus and Stu, a couple of older convicts, renowned for their skills at resolving problems.

Without revealing his concern, Jack asks those assembled, 'By the way, have you seen my wife this morning?'

No-one but Jack, knows that his wife's mother worked for Sir Cecil's father and grandfather back in Gloucestershire. Being a child at the time, no-one in the Billingsworth family recognised her when they took her on as part of their allotment of convicts. Even Jack isn't sure, but he suspects that his wife has revenged her mother's treatment She saw Sir Cecil's father rape her mother. She was only eight years old, but the assault was obvious. It drove her mother insane.

Where she is now, he doesn't know for sure, but he does know that his wife was always kind to the aborigines, always treated them with respect. He can only hope that she is with them, far away from the white men who will do their best to track her down and make her suffer. He has done his duty; the trackers have been sent to look for Sir Cecil's killer. They didn't need to be asked, not to find her.

Call Bell
Alwena Willis

Shocked, Jan just sat there. She glanced at Pete next to her. He looked equally shocked. She looked across at the doctor. 'Are you sure?'

'I'm afraid so; the MRI and other tests confirm it. We would like to make an appointment with a Neurosurgeon and an Oncologist to commence treatment as soon as possible.'

'Can it be cured?' Jan asked since Pete just sat there staring through the window. Who could blame him?. He had just been handed a death sentence at the age of fifty-five? What of their retirement plans, what of their future?

Concentrate, she thought. Don't fall to pieces. Find out all the information to help Pete. That's priority right now. You can fall apart later. She glanced at him again. He hadn't moved an inch.

Over the next half hour, she found out all the ins and outs of the treatment, the referrals and follow up treatment. Overwhelmed, she grabbed Pete's hand, made their way to the car and drove home in complete silence. She didn't try to engage in conversation. He needed time. Time to digest that in a years' time, even with all the aggressive treatment available, he probably would not be alive. How do you come to terms with being given a virtual death sentence?

Over the next year Pete became more and more reclusive, only really wanting to spend time with her or the children. His treatment was harrowing and if it had been left to him, he would not have had it. His daughters, on the other hand, wanted him to have a chance to live even if it was a slim one so begged him to have the treatment, though deep down, he regretted it. He would have loved to live but this was not living so three months into the treatment after being told they would have to repeat it as it was not working as well as they hoped, he had withdrawn from it all, deciding to just enjoy the rest of his remaining life with his wife and family. He chose quality over quantity.

The last few months had been special for her and the children. Andrew, their son, had been up from Busselton for a couple of weeks with his wife and son. Jess, Michelle and Lauren came around daily due to living a couple of streets away. Time was not on Pete's side though and within a matter of months he was admitted to Rosemount Hospice where he received the best of care.

Visiting every day became a habit and this last week she had been advised the time was near and to start staying the nights. Numbness is probably the best way to describe how she felt, and scared. Each night she went to sleep dreading waking up to find him gone and yet part of her prayed he had. Pain is a terrible thing when you see it ravage someone you love. It is heartbreaking. Physically seeing him deteriorate to a fraction of the man he was, brought a sadness to her heart that was beyond words. Her big brave strong husband reduced to a mere whisp of a man in a bed.

They spoke of the good old days, the happy times, the fun times and the emotional times of their lives. They realised they were the fortunate ones, the rare ones in today's world that fell in love when they were young and stayed in love. She supposed many would like to know how they managed it but, in all honesty, she couldn't tell them. Pete was just Pete, who she fell in love with and always loved. Why? Because he was just Pete, her Pete.

The kids came every evening to sit with him and had done so this evening as she had taken the time to nip to the hospice chapel for a weep and a prayer. She prayed every night for the strength to let him go when the time came. How can she let him go? She could cry to God that it's not fair, but nothing in life is and it's not his fault. Instead, she prays for his strength, that is all she can do. She headed back to his room and saw he was already sleepy; he had a hard day today. She sees the pain etched on his face, she sits on the bed and holds his hand.

'You are tired tonight I will let you sleep.'

'Stay here with me until I drop off'

'Of course, I will just stare at your handsome face.'

Pete gave a faint smile. 'Don't be too lonely without me'

Jan looked down at him 'I have no intentions of being lonely, I am going to take up pottery, learn a new language, start playing the piano again, amongst other things. I have also fancied watercolours and I may also do a course on home mechanics. No, I won't have time to be lonely. Don't be too lonely up there while you wait for me either. Obviously, I will be a bit busy for a while so you will just have to be patient okay?'

'Won't you want some companionship?'

'I have the dog and the cat for that and they do as they are told, well most of the time, and don't answer back. Very important. That's all I need until we meet again, Pete.'

He smiled, closed his eyes. 'Good, as long as you are sure, my love. I love you, night, night.'

'Love you too, my love, sleep tight.' She kissed him gently and made her way to the fold up bed.

She stirred as the hand gently shook her and she looked up into a pair of lovely brown, sad, yet resigned eyes. The woman said only two words but they were the last words she wanted to hear. The two words that probably terrified her the most at this moment.

'It's time.'

She looked back at a face full of compassion, a face that more than likely had delivered this message several times before to many other people - all feeling the dread she now felt. She rose, glanced towards the bed and noticed that he was free of all the numerous attachments she was so used to seeing on him. She made a slow way towards the man who had been part of her life for so long and looked down at him. He looked more peaceful than he had for many months. His breathing was shallow, yet noisy, but he seemed to be pain-free at last.

She glanced at Bridget, his nurse. 'May I lay with him for the last time.'

Bridget looked back at her, glanced away quickly. 'Of course, I will leave you to spend these last few moments alone. If you need me, use the call bell.' Bridget walked away turning just once to say, 'Take your time.'

When the nurse left, she slipped onto the bed next to her beloved, and for the last time, wrapped her arms around him. 'You fought bravely, my love. Now go in peace. Don't worry about me or the children. We will be fine. We will always have you in our hearts and remember all the happy times we had together. No one can take those away from us. The children are adults now, making their own way in life and you have taught them well. So go in peace and look out for us from above and wait for me there. There will be no one else for me. It was always just you; it will always be just you. So be patient my love we will be together again one day. Just rest now.'

She didn't know whether he heard her or not or how long she lay there. She knew the moment he passed, but wasn't ready to let him go yet, so continued to hold him close. This man she loved. Her soulmate. After a while the tears slowed, she unwrapped herself from him and looked down at his peaceful face. She gave him one last tender kiss and pressed the call bell.

Teddy and Barbara
Dot Wilson

Teddy warily looked at himself in the mirror, a task made much easier with his new eyes. It had been a long time, decades in fact, since he had had a chance to see himself, and here he was propped up on the settee in front of the trendy new floor mirror which was leaning against the opposite wall in the lounge room. He was very excited to discover how he looked after his trip to the teddy bear repair shop. After years of being dragged around by the nose and being subject to many games of tug-of-war between Barbara and her older brother he knew he was definitely the worse for wear; the stuffing had disappeared from his nose and the stitching was worn. One ear had come off and the other was loose, and one eye was missing. Stuffing was coming out of a large gap in the stitching down his middle, and possibly worst of all, his growler was broken. When he was turned over and back up again there was silence where once there had been an impressive low rumbling noise emanating from the depths of his ample tummy.

Barbara had finally found a teddy bear shop in Subiaco that did repairs; he knew it had been an expensive exercise because he overheard Barbara complaining to her friend, Robyn, about how much it had cost. He was a bit concerned when Barbara put him in the car one day, he hadn't left the house for as long as he could remember, he just sat propped up in various chairs around the house and was subject to the occasional going over with the vacuum cleaner. Every now and again she would place one of her hats on his head: a beanie in winter, and a Santa hat at Christmas time. He imagined he looked very smart, and certainly Barbara's friends said he looked 'so cute' and he felt quite flattered.

He had enjoyed his trip to the repair shop, it was very gratifying to be the centre of so much attention although he did feel a little dowdy when he looked at all the smart brand-new teddies for sale. Some of them looked so soft and fluffy, and there were pink ones and blues ones, and some were wearing very fancy outfits. Things had certainly changed since he had last been on display in a shop. Finally, the tugging and the tweaking and the stuffing and the stitching were all over and Barbara came back to get him. He was very pleased to see her and glad to be going home.

Barbara placed Teddy on the settee and cast a critical eye over her renovated teddy bear. Overall, the woman in the shop had done a pretty good job, although one ear sat lower than the other, but it was nice not to have kapok stuffing coming out of his middle and drifting onto the furniture anymore. She did find his new eyes a little disconcerting for she had been used to his one-eyed look, but she could almost imagine that those new amber orbs with the enormous black pupils were staring into her soul. She could do without that, as there were times when she felt oddly guilty about the wear and tear on her old playmate, as she recalled dragging him around the house by his nose and imagining herself as a surgeon when she attempted to stitch back his ear and sew up his middle seam. The fights with her older brother, Ian, hadn't helped either. Their dad had said that Teddy was originally a present for him, but Teddy was so big that Ian was scared of him, and Barbara had adopted him instead. Ian had always resented that, perhaps that was the beginning of the rift in their relationship, who knew?

The bear was basically a nice adornment to the house now, so repairs had been necessary. Her friends had admired him when they came round one time and she had put a hat on him, but they had teased her about his poor condition, so she had finally succumbed and forked out to get the work done.

She suddenly remembered there was one last thing to check. The growler. The lady in the shop had asked her if she wanted a new one put in. She almost wasn't going to bother and then decided why not, might as well go the whole hog.

She picked Teddy up and turned him onto his tummy then back up again. Oh dear, the faint noise that emanated from his insides wasn't so much like the growl that she remembered but more like the bleating of a sick sheep. Well, that was disappointing. It wasn't worth complaining about as she would in reality never use it, but it had been a waste of money. She sat the bear back on the settee and went into the kitchen to start cooking dinner.

At last, the growl! Teddy was so excited to hear what his new growler sounded like. For a second he had a bird's eye view of the carpet as Barbara turned him over, then she flipped him back and that awful sound came out of him. He was devastated. That wasn't a proper bear's growl at all! He could see Barbara's face and he tried with all his might to convey his disappointment through his new eyes, but she just placed him back on the settee, gave him a little pat on the head and walked away towards the kitchen.

Neil's New Book
Graham Chapman

Neil veered into the Hay Street mall and took aim for Dymocks. It was a brutally hot day and the five-minute walk from Boffins Books had him sweating already. He was excited with his visit to Boffins, as his book was well displayed within Australian fiction along with a Subiaco post review:

> *Peppermint Cove demands attention as this new author uses a brutal midnight murder of Mike the mower-man who moved almost invisibly observing the behaviour of the people of a wealthy suburb. An arrest is just a beginning as an under-resourced police force, pits itself against the resources of power and privilege using Mick's diaries to guide them through the labyrinth of deceit and deception.*
>
> *Vicki Mason, Subiaco Post.*

He was very pleased with the quote as it had taken a meal at Hungry Jacks followed by dinner at Fraser's up at King's Park to convince Vicki his book was worthy of a review. It took her some time to understand his book was not just about crime. It was about injustice, oppression and the veneer of respectability that covered the darker side of elites who lived comfortable and respectable lives, while involved in serious criminal activity and the exploitation of disadvantaged.

The cool rush of the air conditioner wafted over him as he walked into Dymocks. He glimpsed his book in the New Books section only to see the last copy removed by a customer, leaving an empty shelf. He ventured further into the shop where the air was even cooler, to find his books, and perhaps Vicki who was working today. He found Australian fiction - his book was missing! Now anxious, he wandered up and down a few aisles and then went round a corner where a group of men and women were in deep discussion in the

Crime section. They were discussing his book! While quite upset his book was in the Crime section, he somehow noticed the group was growing and there were now over a dozen people talking about his book.

'It's just what we'd expect from those types,' said one woman.

'They have no respect for people out our way.' complained a middle-aged businessman.

Vicki was in the middle of the group encouraging conversation while she facilitated book purchases with her hand-held credit machine.

Vicki caught Neil's eye. While frustrated his books were in Crime, he loved the growing conversation amongst the group. He nodded at Vicki with fondness, and she smiled back, which drew attention to Neil. He smiled warmly at his new fans, took out his pen, and engaged with the now very excited group.

That evening, as they dined at the Charthouse restaurant in South Perth, Neil thanked Vicki for her initiative in placing his book in Crime. He told her the same thing happened to a young Scottish writer who thought his new book was a mainstream Scottish novel in the tradition of Robert Louis Stevenson. Neil described how he was beginning to understand no matter what the intent of his writing, once published, he relinquished control. He had to let go and allow his readers and booksellers to own his story.

Vicki smiled and gently touched his hand. Her eyes sparkled and his heart missed a beat. Neil sensed a new adventure story was about to begin.

She Wolf
Theo Pabst

Demitrius Pravdaski put another log into the small pot-bellied stove in his cabin. This winter was turning out to be one of the worst in memory. He was the only one there occupying the small cabin in the dense forest east of Moscow. He was the owner and editor of a small newspaper in Moscow called Pravda, meaning 'truth and justice.' A royalist, he was not, but he believed in the stability the royal family had given Mother Russia over the years. The peasants did not always share these thoughts and were in the throes of an uprising. They wanted independence from the tyranny of the crown. Anyone with even an inkling of loyalists' thinking would be in grave danger of losing their life. Hence his taking refuge in their cabin. Demitrius and his wife, Volga, had spent many summer days here enjoying the serenity of the forest and living from the land when possible.

They had occupied a two-room apartment overlooking the Kremlin over the Moskva River in Moscow. It was not much, but they were happy. Demitrius would go out each morning and spend time discussing the country's dispositions in the local coffee shops. Then, he would take their stories back to his newspaper office, where he would put them to print. As he went through the door of their apartment, Volga would say to Demitrius, 'Look after yourself now,' which he took with all the love it held.

Volga became pregnant, and the thought of becoming a father left him with great expectations of family life. Then misfortune struck. The baby was ready to be born. The midwife was called, and all the preparations were put into place. Hot water and clean towels were prepared. It was a breech-birth, and by the time the head appeared, it was realised too late that the umbilical cord had wound itself around the baby's neck, cutting off the oxygen and stopping life before it even began. Volga had started to bleed. She asked to hold their child, hoping it might come back to life, not realising that her own was slowly ebbing away. They could not stop the bleeding, and not long after the birth, Volga passed away clutching their son to her chest. That image was imprinted in his mind and would haunt Demetrius forever.

The nights spent in the cabin by himself were the hardest to bear. It was the loneliness that got to him. He missed Volga terribly. The winter had come early, it started to snow. It drove the wolves closer to his cabin, hoping for any food scraps that might have been thrown out. Their howls became more prominent, amplified by the stillness of the night. I will set a trap to discourage them from coming nearer, he thought. One of the first things he did the following day was to check on the trap he had set to see whether it had worked. From a distance, he could see it had done its job, for a wolf's outline was visible. Approaching it carefully, he was stopped by a voice coming from somewhere. He looked around him but could not see anyone there.

'Well, will you just stand there like a dummy or set me free? I will be indebted to you for the rest of my life if you do. I am not used to having a broken leg, so I cannot fend for myself.'

Demitrius turned around, faced the wolf, and said, 'Did you just say something to me?'

'Well, who else could it be, as we are the only ones here.'

'But wolves can't speak.'

'As you can hear, this one can, so please take note.'

Demitrius stood there dumbfounded. 'You expect me to set you free with no guarantees that you'll either bite me or run off.'

'Have you ever tried to run with three legs? No. Neither have I. Sometimes, you must trust someone, and this could be your first time.'

After evaluating the situation, he turned to the wolf and said, 'I will release you on one condition: you will join me in my cabin.'

'Have you got a fire in there?'

'Yes.'

'Well, what are you waiting for? It is cold out here, and my leg is aching, something chronic.'

He undid the trap, lifted the wolf, and took it inside the cabin. After cleaning the wound with vodka and applying a splint and bandage, he laid the wolf on an old rug next to the pot-belly stove.

'One could get used to this,' the wolf stated and rolled over, warming both sides of its body. 'What is for dinner? Now, would that be stretching the boundaries too far?'

As it happened, Demitrius had snared a few hares a few days ago, and skinned and prepared them for the pot. There would be enough for both for the time being.

'Do you have a family?' he asked of the wolf.

'I used to, but some young whippersnapper challenged my mate last winter to take over the pack and he won. He banished me because I was the oldest and most useless. I was checking out your cabin, hoping to find some food. What about you?'

'I had a wife, but I lost her after giving birth to our stillborn son. Also, my political views were not appreciated by the masses. That is why I am here alone, avoiding it all.'

'Well, that makes us a pigeon pair. We could even grow old together.'

'Now it might be alright for you, for you have only a few years left to live where I have half a lifetime ahead of me, so don't include me in your scheme of things.'

It had been a long day for Demitrius, one he still could not fully comprehend. He put another log into the potbelly stove and closed the grate so it would last the night out and leave some embers for the morning. Did a wolf talk to him, or was it all in his imagination? He looked along the stove, where the wolf was fast asleep chasing God-knows-what in its dreams. He resigned to the fact, for it must have happened, and accepted it all. He found his bed and collapsed onto it. Sleep overtook him within seconds, and his dreams engulfed him.

He awoke the following day and went to the pot-belly stove with a fresh log to place on last night's embers, re-energising the fire to a warm glow. Today, Demitrius felt more at ease after yesterday's introduction to a talking wolf. He was either going mad or, for some unknown reason, had been singled out to have the privilege of being able to talk to wolves.

There on the floor beside the stove lay the wolf fast asleep. So, I was not dreaming after all, he thought. It would be nice to have some company this winter, even if it is only a wolf. It seems to be able to hold a reasonable conversation.

The pot with one of the hares, wild roots, salt and some herbs, went onto the stove, where it would slowly cook for the rest of the day, ready for tonight's meal. It would be nice to share it with someone, even a wolf.

The wolf woke, shook its head, and unruffled its coat. It hobbled over to Demitrius on three legs and said, 'I know you set that trap to catch me, and you could have left me out there to die, but you did not. Then you took me in, patched me up, and gave me a warm place to sleep and food to heal me. For all that, I feel indebted towards you, and I hope to be able to repay you in some way.'

In retrospect, the wolf could communicate with him in spades, which became its repayment. It would ensure that Demetrius kept his sanity that winter.

At night, with a full stomach, a glass of Vodka for him, clean water for her, and a warm fire close by, they would sit there for hours, discussing all types of subjects he was sure no wolf should have any knowledge of — but somehow did. There were times during their musings Demitrius felt a closeness towards the wolf, which he could not explain. The wolf slotted into their debates specific characteristics, phrases, and even words that were only privy to him and Volga.

Their companionship continued for the duration of the winter. The wolf's leg healed, which meant it could help put food on the table. They enjoyed each other's company and had many stories to tell. But as the days grew warmer and the pot belly was not used as much, the yearning for the outside world became more vital for the wolf. She had appreciated the man's company more than he would ever know, but now she needed to return to her environment and way of life and for him to regain his position in life in Moscow.

'Look after yourself now,' Volga said to Demitrius, tongue in cheek. If wolves could smile, there would have been one on her face. She turned away from him and the cabin, and slowly walked into the forest, disappearing into the undergrowth. She had done her job.

One will never know whether they met again. But Demitrius had survived the long winter with his sanity due to the company of a wolf who had shared his cabin. It was now up to him to go back to Moscow to fight through print for what he thought was right.

Alpha Male
Theo Pabst

He was the most magnificent specimen of his type, sitting proudly in front of his den. His fur shone in the warm afternoon sunlight. Chunks were missing from his ears and one lip. These honours had been well and truly earned while he defended himself against challenges from the up-and-coming young beta cubs. Nothing pleased him more than watching his children play, making the most of their young and learning days. 'Ah, to be back and be one of them,' he thought.

He stood and felt the returning twinge in his back as he did. This was not the first time he had felt it, for it had become more frequent than he liked. I must be getting old he thought, leaving it to that.

During one of his afternoon inspections of the family group, he heard a now familiar growl of a beta-male wanting to challenge him. Not again, he thought. Can't they leave me alone and let me live the rest of my life in peace? He puffed up his chest and turned around to face his adversary as he had done on many occasions. Before him stood a splendid opponent, almost a replica of his younger self. Was it one of his grandsons? Had it come to this to be confronted with one of your own?

This was not the time to delve into the unknown, as his survival was being tested. His sound-trusted technique had let his opponent make the first move. For some unknown reason, he diverted from the norm, led the attack, and regretted it because his back did not want to follow his instructions. It finished up being a half-hearted attempt by him. His opponent saw the opportunity and took full advantage. Both gave their utmost towards the encounter.

We all know there can only be one winner in any challenge. Unfortunately, the time had come for a new leader to lead the family, leaving the defeated to retreat and live the rest of his life the best way he could.

He had not planned it this way, but he knew it would eventually end this way sometime in his life. He had seen others thrust into this situation and wondered how they survived.

Now, it was his turn.

Forest Fly Reveals Murderer
Janusz Zejdler

Amidst the tranquillity of a serene Sunday afternoon, a storm was brewing in a world divided between a lush forest and an oval-shaped lake. This idyllic setting, once a sanctuary for nature enthusiasts, had transformed over the years, blending natural beauty with the resources of the forest and lake. It had prospered, catering to the needs of its inhabitants and accumulating wealth, which was evident in its thriving businesses and residential structures.

One feature that drew attention was not the property size but the garden surrounding it. It was a professional work of art, a testament to the owner's love of gardening. The front of the house faced the garden while the lake provided a stunning sunset each evening, best enjoyed from the back veranda - a perfect spot to unwind with a glass of wine and snacks after a day's activities. The sun descended towards the west, casting its brilliance on the lake where locals enjoyed small yachts, swimming or fishing. Those on the banks were starting to pack up, ready to head home, adding a touch of realism to the idyllic scene.

The external view of the property gave the impression everything was glowing throughout. But people can have a façade, which, if it is not discovered in time, can lead to a bad outcome. And so it was in this instance. The man, the owner of this beautiful property, was not just wrestling with a profound internal conflict, one that threatened to shatter the peace and beauty of his surroundings. His internal turmoil was a cyclone, a storm about to break. One could almost feel the tension in the air.

Everything was not well for within the house was evidence of aggressive disagreement. There was crying and shouting about a lack of empathy for their troubled situation, no-one considering or accepting who was at fault. The tension in the air was palpable. And then, gradually, the disagreement ceased, leaving a lingering unease and a promise of more.

A man appeared from the rear of the house. He ambled towards the lake foreshore and mingled with the crowd, stopped to chat here and there. He progressed towards the watery growth until he vanished into it. His thoughts were still with the ugly behaviour at home and the way it ended. There was no going home tonight; it would only re-ignite the conflict, and he didn't want this to happen.

Going past a store, he purchased food for his evening meal and remembered the batteries for his torches were flat, so he acquired these as well. He hoped being away from each other for a time would give them time to reflect and rationally reconsider the deterioration of their marriage. He headed towards his destination in the forest, a secluded spot with a small clearing and a comfortable log for sitting, his place of solace, where he could find peace and clarity amidst the chaos of his life.

At the house, the sun neared the horizon, and while there was still some daylight left, a woman appeared, taking care that no one saw her. Her appearance was not that expected of one who was naturally attractive and took care of herself. The disputes, especially the recent one, had taken a toll. She resolved that she was not going to put up with the arguments any longer. It was time to put an end to this nonsense. She headed towards the lake. After a stroll along the shore, deep in thought, she suddenly looked up and saw that the day was ending. She increased her speed. So as not to become lost, she had to reach her destination before complete darkness took over. She had been in this forest before but was unsure exactly what, or where, to look.

It was not until much later that evening a figure stole towards the house. With the clouds covering the moon, it was easy to keep under cover, over the fence, through the garden shrubbery, and towards the back of the house. There were no lights to indicate anyone's presence.

The couple met at a social after their university graduation ceremony. With the social activities in full swing, a misunderstanding occurred over who would dance with whom. While pushing and pulling at one another, one of the girls fell over, and whoever caused it was taken to task by a sharp punch. When it looked like it would be a free-for-all, a young man, stepped in. He was the wrestling and weightlifting university champion. His actions were not aggressive, just a confident, positive move to restore order. It was a gentle approach to separate those who were causing the hassle. Soon, all was back to normal.

The young man helped himself to a glass of bubbly and went outside. The full moon showed off its magic beams across the garden. Admiring the beauty of the evening with his dreams of the future and what it might hold for him, his distant thoughts were interrupted by a goddess standing before him.

'Is the seat next to you reserved for someone, or can anyone take it?'

He just looked at her unable to find words to answer. 'What is your name?' he eventually said as he looked at the seat. 'Please take it. I did not expect the moon to be so prompt with my wishes by sending you down here on its light beam. Can I get you a glass of champagne?'

She was about his height, with a shapely figure and light brown hair. They spent the evening sharing what they hoped to achieve in the future and where it might take them. Strangely, both qualified in accounting and hoped to establish a business somewhere in a place each had dreamed of. Both wanted to look for a place where forests and lakes were close. That special moonbeam had brought them together that evening.

They went their separate ways, wishing their paths might cross in the not-too-distant future. The young man went looking for a place close to forests and lakes. He stayed where he could get a job with an accounting firm to obtain practical experience. With savings, he moved from a motorbike to an excellent motorcar, which showed prestige—looking for a permanent position. As luck would have it, he found the vacancies in a local paper. He noticed a conference was in place close to where he lived. This was just the place to mingle with opportunities for a position. He took the temptation and submitted his expression of interest without delay.

The goddess went home to where her parents lived. The town was exactly what she liked. It had a forest and a lake and opportunities for a new profession in accountancy. Initially, as an employee, she gained practical experience and, as time passed, built her own business. She established her personal and leadership skills, and participated in social activities, especially swimming and sailing small yachts on the lake. Young men were interested in her friendship, but she didn't respond.

On the day of the conference, he arrived early to ensure an excellent place to hear the speaker's presentation. It was a big gathering with people from different districts. He approached the registration desk and gave his name. The young lady looked up and asked again for his name. This time, their eyes met, and there was a moment of magic. Both excused themselves for staring at each other, and the registration continued.

When the official part was over and the social part took place, people wandered with drinks in their hands in search of others who may have been interested in what took place. The young man went outside to get fresh air and digest the things mentioned. His mind returned to the registration *magic moment*.

Where had he seen that girl before? She looked so familiar, or was it just a wishful thought?

Just then, an almost familiar voice from behind spoke. 'What? No fights to break up? If you like, I will go and start one?'

'No,' he said. 'You stay here and never leave me. I recognise the moonlight goddess sent to me that graduation evening. Every full moon, I sit outside and wait for her to appear, but she never did until now. I tried contacting you but didn't know where to look. And here you are.' And there he stopped, apologising for his direct approach 'You are not married or engaged, are you?'

She looked at him and smiled. 'No, I am not married or engaged. I am too busy creating an empire and waiting for you to arrive. I always thought we would meet up, and we did in my hometown.'

They married and established their accounting firm. They built a beautiful home with an excellent garden and enjoyed their happy and prosperous life. High-profile local citizens and people from other areas celebrated happy occasions at their place. The couple wanted their lifestyle with their mind on the town's business and social engagement. They noticed lately that wherever they went, there were always children. So, one Sunday afternoon, whilst on the lake enjoying pleasant yachting, the question came up about starting a family. They agreed, and plans were made. There were sufficient rooms for a nursery, and when the time came for domestic help and at-work casual support whilst the *moon goddess* was nursing the baby.

The planning and actions for their wish to happen were easy. However, a year went by with no results. It was not for a lack of trying. There was sincere love in their efforts, and they both gave and received pleasure. Doubts began to take place.

Why?

What are we doing wrong?

Who is at fault and why?

Such questions came more frequently and, at times, were aggressive. The ongoing feud created tension between them, with no-one outside their home being aware. It began to get ugly and seemed to worsen as time went on. The only noticeable behaviour was that the husband spent more time in the forest or the middle of the lake. Equally, the wife was in her bedroom with a closed door. This made it even worse.

Working from home suited them and their business. It saved daily travelling to and from work. They did not interact much with the locals apart from business requirements. They were not spiritual and seldom attended their local church, and with no children, there were no school links with parents in any related activities. Even with their respective relatives, contact was infrequent. There was no outside social contact except those connected with their professional lives, and little was known about their married-life situation.

And now, this late summer afternoon, just as the sun set in the west, unnoticed by anyone, the wife left the house.

On his return from the forest, the husband found his wife was gone, and after waiting a while, he went to the neighbours to see if she was there. Then he called the wife's parents and, when that failed, the police.

It was unusual for someone to disappear for no apparent reason. No strangers were reported in the village, and there was no reported or observed out-of-character behaviour from or by the couple. Following an intense search of the forest and the lake by police divers and extended enquiries in neighbouring towns, there were no sightings of the missing person. The police turned to the husband because he had visited the forest, but after unsuccessful results from the police interview, the case became a cold case.

The village was not the same from that time on. The once evident trust among them was no longer there. Parents walked with their children or other children in groups. As time passed, the strict attention to safety eased, and the town returned to its previous self. The abandoned husband was considered innocent and had nothing to do with her unusual disappearance. He gradually became involved in the village social activities and became popular in certain events. He became attracted to a lady his age who was equally interested in similar activities. Their relationship grew, and before long, there were wedding bells. And to his very great surprise, there were children. To him, it confirmed it was not his fault but his first wife.

Once clear of the foreshore, the wife followed the fire smoke closer to where it was coming from. The shelter amongst the bushes was not easy to find, except for the giveaway smoke. Moving like a hunter after its prey, she snuck close until she could see what was happening on the inside. And there he was with a fire to keep him warm, a battery lamp to read his book, but what brought her to her limits of self-control was the bottle of wine and a glass, and suddenly, the frightening thought, was there was someone else? Was he, during all that time, cheating on her whilst she was sitting at home crying her eyes out?

Without thought, she rushed in and yelled what she thought of him, hitting him with her fist. Before he realised what was happening, he was on the floor trying to defend himself.

She was much stronger than he thought. He always had a short fuse, and it lit up. He began to defend himself by attacking her. He grabbed her by the throat and held her with all his strength. She realised he had lost control and was going to kill her.

She yelled out, pleading with him not to kill her. He could only hear the sound, not the words and just looked down on her, not easing his grip. She muttered repeatedly, saying he would never get away with it.

He spat rage through gritted teeth. 'Who is going to stop me here? No one knows.'

Just then, a forest fly flew past. The wife looked at it and said, 'This fly is a witness and will one day reveal to the world what you have done, and you will be charged with my murder.' And with these last dying words on her lips, she lost consciousness and went limp.

There was a deafening silence; the only noise was the wind moving gently through the trees, shaking their leaves to attract attention to what had just happened. The wind continued to spread the message through the forest. It continued until the sun rose, welcoming a brand-new day.

When the husband realised what had taken place, he stood, took his head between his hands, gave one hell of a scream like a wounded animal, and collapsed. When he came to his senses, he panicked. What to do with the body? Self-preservation was the conclusion. He remembered that close by was a sizeable thick bush of berries, and behind this, unknown to anyone around the village, was a bottomless soak of quicksand.

He went to it and removed the top cover of dead leaves, half-rotten branches, and overgrowth. Placing the body gently on top of the soak, he allowed it to sink slowly until it disappeared. He then carefully replaced the material he had removed. To ensure it kept the body down, he placed a log on top. No-one would ever look inside the thick berry bushes. Even if they did, they would overlook the clay soak in the middle. He went back to the shack and carefully ensured there was no evidence of his wife ever being there or any unusual or violent behaviour. Satisfied, her went home as normal as possible, established his wife's absence from home - her most extraordinary act of absence.

The full moon shone brightly, penetrating the thick bush of berries, reaching the hidden burial place and lighting up the resting place. With the aid of the gentle breeze, the moonlight used the shadows of branches and leaves to paint creative images of live creatures. Creatures that moved to comfort the victim. The nightly warm and moist temperature created evaporation, and the mist surrounded the bush and, with moonlight shining on it, provided a beautifully bright mausoleum for the victim who had her life taken from her so cruelly. In the distance, sounds of crying wolves and barking foxes, late-feeding deer moving slowly and stopping when close to the berry bush. Loud bison and elk competed with their voices. The night owls join with other fauna, offered sympathy for what had occurred. But when the sun appeared on the horizon, everything was back to normal in the forest, as if nothing had happened. There was a new welcoming day for everyone to enjoy.

The reason for the first wife's absence was never explained, nor the location of her body was ever found. The husband's second marriage and a new family of four children were incredibly happy.

But picnics do not always end in happiness. During one, there was a single annoying fly that would not go away. It irritated the man with its pestering. The new wife, noticing his unusual behaviour, tried to calm him, which brought about an uncommon reaction. Suddenly, he stopped and began to laugh, not his typical humour but an uncontrolled frenzy.

The wife was troubled why the fly brought this unusual reaction. Later, she asked him about it but he didn't respond other than to make an excuse for losing his cool because of the stupid fly. She persisted over the next few days, concerned that it may affect her husband's well-being.

Eventually, he gave in, after making her promise not to tell anyone what he was about to reveal to her. He figured it had been too many years since the episode occurred for any action against him could be possible. He revealed to her what took place and the episode with the fly, which his first wife predicted would lead to conviction of his act of committing the murder. He also told her how clever he was in hiding the body, which would have sunk to the bottom of the clay soak by now.

After hearing the story, the wife was troubled about what her husband was capable of, her future well-being, and the children's. After thinking the situation through, she called the police and let them decide what action to take. The husband fully cooperated with the law and brought them to the spot where the body was. To his utter surprise, the body was located and retrieved. When placed in the clay soak, it landed on top of the tree trunk, sunk just below the top of the soak and was out of sight from above.

No-one went there. It was a taboo place for the locals. Stories told by the older folks of screams coming from the forest during the night and unexplainable fire tongues flickering above the soak inside the berry bush grove. No one was ever brave enough to investigate. The husband knew the screams were none other than animals that strayed from their path and into the soak. Unable to get out of it, they screamed whilst being drowned by the mix of the poisonous chemical liquid in the soak. The flickering of fire tongues was the escaping gases once mixed with oxygen.

The body was still in good condition, preserved by a thick mix of the soak's contents. There was a funeral attended by the village and neighbouring villagers. The story circulated of the victim's prediction of how the murderer would be apprehended and brought to justice by a small forest fly.

A Sunday Ramble the Devils Way
Alwena Willis

Anna looked at Jeanie. 'Who's idea of a fundraiser was this anyway? I'm sure Vicar Hoyle didn't agree.'

'Not only did he agree, he is joining us. Look.' Jeanie pointed.

Flabbergasted, Anna looked at where Jeanie was pointing and sure enough, there he was, standing amongst the organising crew, with a half a pint of bitter in his hand. Anna knew he was passionate about getting the mini bus for the youth club, but she was surprised at his participation. Especially in this particular fundraiser, which had the potential of something disastrous happening for sure. Though, on thinking about it, he had raised most of the money when he went on the quiz show. For a vicar that was strange enough, and now they only needed to raise £600 more and the van was theirs.

Anna's thoughts came to an abrupt halt when Jeanie spoke. 'Right, we are off soon. First stop - *The White Lion.*'

Yes, believe it or not this was a fundraising pub crawl with the aim to raise the last of the money for the minivan. From the look of it the whole village was out here and therefore it was a no- brainer to be a success. There were even some people here from the neighbouring villages of Woodborough and Oxton. The MC, Fred, from *The Gleaners*, held everyone's attention which was difficult with the crowd spilling out into the car park. With his trusty microphone, he relayed the rules. In groups of twenty they would make their way either clockwise or anti-clockwise around the streets of Calverton via its pubs. There they would purchase a drink and get their card stamped and after fifteen minutes, move on to the next pub. They would rotate through until they were back here at the *Gleaners Inn.* All fully stamped cards could then receive a drink at half price on their return. There would be a band playing in the gardens and the after-party would start. The amount of money raised would be announced at eight o clock and make sure everyone is on their best behaviour. A comment that was met with a lot of boos and heckling.

Two groups would leave every fifteen minutes and Jeanie and I were in the first group. On the sound of the horn, off we went with much laughter and merriment.

The *White Lion* was our first stop. Jeanie purchased us a half pint of larger each and a packet of cheese and onion crisps. The pub was busy and Jeanie and I wondered how the husbands were faring, watching the children at home. We both giggled at the thought, the husbands lost the toss of who would do the pub crawl. They would meet us later when the baby sitters arrived.

The bell went and we downed the last of the larger and headed for the *Admiral Rodney*, a very short walk away. Now it must have taken all of three minutes to walk there but the fresh air certainly had an effect on us.

My turn and I purchased a Bacardi and coke each. Jeanie questioned why I was mixing the drinks. I just said one word, 'bladder.' She understood perfectly. Now we were conscious of how we giggled more than usual, and presumed it was the atmosphere. Cards stamped once more, bell rang, off we all poured out to the next stop *The Cherry Tree*. Now this entailed a slightly longer walk of maybe ten minutes, which soon passed with a lot of laughing, cars beeping as the group spilled onto the road, jumping back onto the pavement as the irate drivers were honking their horns. We were beginning to become quite a loud group and, in the distance, we could hear the laughter of the second group which made us giggle more. The fact that most people knew each other meant there was a camaraderie, which made it more of a fun night.

As we entered *The Cherry Tree*, the music hit us and Jeanie and I did what we always did and headed for the dance floor. How wonderful to forget we were young mothers for a few minutes and pretend we were young, free and slightly wild again. After two dances Jeanie quickly rushed to the bar for two more Bacardi and cokes as we barely had five minutes to finish the drink before the bell would go. We downed the drink and ended back on the dance floor for one more dance.

I must admit we were tempted to give the pub crawl up and just stay there to dance but as Jeanie so eloquently slurred, 'We're not qui-quitters are we?' and in the condition I was in it sounded perfectly right to me. So, cards stamped, we all rolled out of *The Cherry Tree* and headed for the *Miners Welfare*. I must admit walking back down Manning Road towards the club, the cool breeze hit us like a blast from the North Pole and somehow our walking seemed to slow. We walked arm-in-arm to keep ourselves warm, but it was more like to keep ourselves upright.

We went with larger again at the *Welfare* and walked into a lot of cheering and clapping from the regulars. Having purchased the lager's, we flirted with some of the older miners who were friends of our dad's and we laughed a lot and enjoyed ourselves. It felt like we were only there two minutes when the bell went and it was time to go again. Once more we had to scull our drinks, which was not a good idea, but with lots of encouragement from the regulars, we did.

Clutching our stamped cards, we stumbled outside and headed for the *Working Men's Club*, affectionally called the *Geordie Club*. This was again just a short walk but nearly everyone in the group were struggling including the diehard drinkers.

We staggered into the *Geordie Club* to gasps and laughter from the regulars. At this stage the bladder was priority and the drinks second so of course this ate into our fifteen minutes. After a quick trip to the ladies, we went with Bacardi and coke again, which took less time to drink. We sat leaning on each other, grinning at everyone and wondering how an earth we were going to walk back to the *Gleaners Inn* to finish the pub crawl. Just when we were contemplating this the bell rang and so we got up and limped outside, down Manning Road and tumbled left onto Main Street, waving at probably the last group entering *The Whie Lion*. Many of our group redistributed their drinks along the way, in people's gardens. Jeanie and I had a small stop perched on the church wall for a few minutes before we got a second wind and practically crawled back to finish at the *Gleaners*.

On arrival, the band was playing, *Congratulations*. Buoyed up by our achievements, we went in for our half price drink.

That is the last thing I can honestly say I remember of the night. Apparently, Hubby duly came, took me home and put me to bed. Jeanie's husband did the same for her. Now I know you are all wondering how Vicar Hoyle fared. He apparently was perfectly fine and partied with everyone afterwards which makes me suspect he must be a closet drinker. The fundraiser did remarkably more than expected as the regulars dipped into their pockets and donated as well. So, with the entrance fees for the pub crawl and donations from participating pubs and the regulars, the grand total raised was £847.50. The minivan was ours or rather the youth clubs.

With hindsight, going in and out of pubs is not recommended if you want to drink. There is something about the cold air hitting you, that enhances the alcohol's effect. Either drink at home as obviously Vicar Hoyle does, or stay in one pub. And as to whose idea it was for a fundraiser, that would have been me. I have told Jeanie to not let me say anything at the next community meeting or raise my hand. But then again, the whole village did love it!

In the Shadows
Nicole Corsini

Tears fell as Georgia began to pack the last of her gran's things into a box. There wasn't a whole lot to pack. The entire contents of her life had been reduced to fit inside one small bedroom that contained a chest of four drawers, small wardrobe, a single bed, one bedside table and a small recliner chair. She opened the top drawer and found an old black and white photo of her grandparents on their wedding day. She looked at it for only a second before she ripped it in half and threw the half of her grandad straight in the bin, then placed the other half into the box.

From the corner of her eye she saw someone walk into the room. Worried they might have seen what she had just done, she looked towards them but no one was there. A sigh of relief left her body before she resumed emptying the drawers. The sensation that someone was there didn't go away though. Her back tingled with the sense of being watched, but from where, she couldn't tell. It came from everywhere in the room.

Desperate to get out of there as soon as possible, she threw what was left in the drawers into the box, not bothering to look at any of it or tape it shut. She tucked the large box awkwardly under her arm, grabbed the rubbish bag then left the nursing home without looking back.

It was ridiculous to imagine some spectre had entered the room but it wasn't the first time she'd experienced such an uncanny sensation. The first had been three weeks ago, during the last visit with her gran. When she arrived, Gran was sitting in the armchair in the corner of the room. It had been turned towards the window so she was able to look at something other than the dull bedroom walls where she spent most hours of the day.

Georgia greeted her with a light kiss on the cheek. 'Hi Gran, how are you feeling today?' She made sure to ask every time, though even on her good days, Gran rarely communicated. This time, she looked frailer than ever before and a shadow seemed to surround her, as if the grim reaper lurked in the darkness, a constant reminder that death was not far away. The thought of it suffocated Georgia and made her want to leave. Instead she ignored the internal voice telling her to run, told herself she was imagining things and to stay focussed on Gran.

The nursing home was always short-staffed, so things like housekeeping often got overlooked. Georgia busied herself with changing the bed sheets, while filling Gran in on how her day was. As she put on the last pillow case and threw the dirty sheets in the washing basket, she looked towards Gran and saw tears fall silently down her cheeks. Her lips moved as if trying to speak but nothing audible escaped. Georgia moved around the bed and knelt next to her, taking her delicate wrinkled hands in her own.

'It's okay Gran, I'm right here,' she whispered. 'Let's get you into bed, I'll sit with you until you fall asleep.' There was no response, as expected.

Georgia put her weight under Gran's arms to help steady her out of the armchair. They shuffled over to the bed. Gran didn't say a word, only moved where she was guided. She had lost so much weight it was easy for Georgia to manoeuvre her onto the bed and under the covers.

It was hard to see her grandma so frail, even after many years of watching the disease steal everything that made Gran who she was. It still broke Georgia's heart. She could clearly remember the day they got the life altering diagnosis - Alzheimer's, ironically on the anniversary of her grandad's death. Ironic because the day he died was the day Gran got her life back. He was an abusive bastard, who had made her life a living hell for thirty-seven years.

To get the news on the same date, ten years later, almost felt like he had come back to haunt them. Georgia blamed all those years of stress as the reason for Gran's brain disease which made her hate him even more.

'I'll be there in the chair until you fall asleep.' Georgia planted another kiss, this time on her gran's forehead. 'I love you so much, Gran.' She lingered for a few moments and waited for a response she knew wouldn't come, then made herself comfortable in the chair. When she was sure her beloved grandma ran was asleep, she quietly left the room, shutting the door behind her.

Mr Poppy
Garry Davies

And in the corner of everybody's eye, as if it were impossible to wish away, even in all the hopeful tussle of cleats on the field, the kicked mud and grass, is Mr Poppy in his wool army coat, out near the goalpost, clapping with his mouth open, urging on the team. In the gasping spirit of the game, all the parents try to forget him.

Andrew Sean Greer, *Life is Over There*

He was a presence that was not easily wished away. The more he was ignored, the more he filled their minds, the effort required to make him invisible could not be contained, it overflowed from them, bogging them down where they stood. And the edges of Mr Poppy's world, over there by the goalpost, flowed out from him and turned them all into islands surrounded by his essence. He became the essential Mr Poppy, seen but not present, present but not seen. He was only partially there, like a mistake, sometimes forgiven, or sometimes forgotten but rarely both.

He was there, every week for two hours as the game flowed on. After it was over the parents collected the happy and thoughtless heroes, along with the younger spectator children, and herded them back out of the playing fields. Some quickly loaded their laughing and muddy offspring into cars which were full of kids, balls and boots and rushed away to the next opportunity of life-affirming pressure. Others — the time rich — formed familiar groups to talk about the week gone or the week to come. They shared the false closeness of friendships forced together by circumstance. Groups bonded by hope or aspiration but condemned to be temporary, ships passing, and knowing this inwardly, they expressed outwardly even more vehemently the closeness of the temporary connection. The false laughs; the extensive touching gestures; the wide-eyed looks revealing to those who could see, the emptiness upon which this world was built.

This empty world shut Mr Poppy out. The world which did not notice the precious essence of life being lived away, spent thoughtlessly and carelessly as though that well — the well of life — had no bottom. The happy, mindless flow of life, the energy put into a boy's game of football, time spent without thought or care, never to be recalled, that world shut Mr Poppy out. The world which lived shut him out. The life-affirming world shut him out.

Mr Poppy, too, had once tasted from the well of an endless life, and it had left its hopes. He too, was once made to think that life could not run out. It made even more bitter the taste of knowing that it did. His boy did not play at this field anymore, but still he came. The faces changed, the coaches, the supporters all changed. They were familiar, and Mr Poppy could see the missing face, as well as the carefree living ones.

Then, one weekend, a woman came to the game with Mr Poppy. They stood by the goalpost, together, clapping and cheering. The boys played on, still spending their lives with thoughtless abandon. But the essence of Mr Poppy had changed. It now flowed in a different direction.

The woman had a certain gravity about her, she must have, because the stream of invisibility no longer flowed quite as strongly from Mr Poppy. It was diverted by the tidal pull of another force — a gravity of light and life. A gravity of presence.

Mr Poppy was discovering that *he* had closed the door of life on himself. The force of the woman was pulling it open, and perhaps at the same time, closing the door which led to loss. The missing face was being allowed to leave the field.

As they left that day, a small white bird fell out of the sky and dropped on the boot-kicked mud and grass of the empty playing field. No-one saw it fall. And no-one was there to see it flutter a moment or two later and rise again into the sky.

The Scenario

An Onlooker's Point of View
Theo Pabst

It was a night I seriously wanted to forget, for my bender had surpassed any I had before, leaving me still dressed her on the couch with the searing summer sun streaming through the open curtains on my already wet perspiring body. It left me with a head the size of a medicine ball, and you could have smoother the most challenging piece of timber with my raspy tongue. The near-empty bottle of whiskey stood on the small table beside me, reminding me of my mother's words: 'Everything in moderation, Son.' Sure, mum, but you have not endured what I suffered to get here.

I slowly got up, letting my head catch up with the rest of my body. I discarded my sodden clothes and amble naked into the shower. I turned the faucet to full and let the cold water cascade over my lifeless body, hoping for some resurrection to occur. It took time for a tiny flicker of life to return to my body. I dressed in my favourite shorts and a provocative T-shirt, hoping it would give me a head-up start to the day.

The thought of food seemed to be least on my mind, but on seeing me, Joe, the owner of the eatery across the road, would know precisely my needs, for he knew me well. Seeing me in this condition, my pick-me-up would be in ready hands before I entered.

I donned sunglasses and a cap and ventured outside into the unbearable heat. The smell of melting asphalt welcomed me and I persevered with its invasion. The fog in my brain was slowly dissipating, releasing me to my supportive surroundings bit by bit.

I lifted my right foot, ready to cross the busy road. Whoosh. A black sedan raced past. It would have taken my foot off if I'd planted it. Before I could follow the car's dramatic flight, there was an almighty crunch of collapsing metal. I turned my head in that direction. Only metres away, a third of the way up the wooden lamp post, the remnants of the sedan hung precariously, an arm swung out from one of the mangled windows.

My half-comatose mind had trouble comprehending the situation in front of me. All I could manage in a strangled voice was, 'Help, help anyone. Please help?'

A Pedestrian's Point of View
Janusz Zejdler

It's the day I've long awaited: I can have my favourite lunch - a barbecue with the aroma of sizzling steak, chopped onions, and slices of pork belly. With a choice to quench the thirst with either a glass of red or Swan draft beer. Maybe a bottle of white in a bucket of ice to keep it cool. Add a selection of greens to choose instead of the onions. All are set, food is ready, drinks are in their handy cool containers, some appropriate music is available, and a TV station is set for when the footy starts. All that is needed now is to start the gas barbie and get the show rolling. Now, to light it with matches from the kitchen. Matches in hand light the barbeque. Adjusting the heat, the flames went out. Bloody hell. Back to the kitchen for the matches. Despite many efforts, no luck. A cold feeling goes through me. No gas.

But all is not lost. Just down the road, near the crossroads, there's a roadside eatery. A place I've frequented many times, known for its delicious food and drinks, including wine and Swan draft beer. The eatery is well-catered, with indoor and outdoor seating in a beautifully maintained garden. It attracts many customers all year round. It's only a short walk away. Not that I need to work up an appetite, but a stroll in the fresh summer air could do me some good. And who knows, maybe some of my football friends will be there.

With my keys and wallet in a small shoulder bag, a slow walk allows me to enjoy nature: the farmer's fields, native shrubs and trees in flower or showing new leaves. Shrieking crows fly in all directions.

There is a lot of traffic on the road: a mix of heavy road trains, other day-to-day transport, and your everyday motorist. Some will stop at the intersection eatery for a bite. It's interesting to see how certain of them follow the supposed rules of the road. It is a three-line highway and should be a safe journey for those using it.

Two cars catch my attention. One was a sporty red MG with an open roof, which on a summery warm day is just perfect. Driving it is a middle-aged gentleman on the lookout for attention for his sexy means of transport. It caught my attention because of the car and how he drove it. I could see myself in it. The other one is a black sedan which seems to be changing lanes too often and too fast.

I near my destination but have to cross the highway to reach the eatery. The traffic had become heavy. I watched, waited for the density to reduce. The traffic seemed to slow when a couple of cars turned into the eatery over a bridge which spans a two-metre-deep ravine near the entry.

I evaluate the oncoming traffic from the left. Some distance back, there is a break of about three car lengths in the lane next to me. The next lane is about the same, so I take the chance to cross. A quick look to my left. All clear. I cross two lanes.

Out of nowhere, the black sedan in the far lane did a sharp left across the two lanes. At the same time, a car in the lane turned into the eatery. I stumble almost safely across. Going way too fast, the black sedan slams on the brakes, skids and smashes into the street lamp post. At the same time I jump to the left – into the ravine below. The smell of tyres burning on the bitumen, the squeal of brakes and crunch of metal couldn't drown out the scream from the car.

Lucky for me, the ravine sides are covered by growth, and the moist, soft ground prevents severe injuries.

The next thing I remember I'm being taken out of the ravine on a stretcher. There is a woman hovering over me. I must be dead and in heaven. This beautiful angel was giving me mouth-to-mouth resuscitation. It's such a lovely feeling, so I reciprocate. She stops.

'This man is definitely not dead. He needs a clean-up and check for any injuries.'

A Diner's Point of View
Tania Park

It is such a delight to get out after a bout of flu. The sun's warmth on my back sends a tingle of pleasure across my shoulders even though a slight breeze keeps the heat at bay. Any time later in the day and the air will be too hot to sit outdoors. I send my friend opposite a smile despite the fact she was the one who spread her germs. At least we are both now rid of the dreaded lurgy.

Behind her, the intersection is busier than normal for an early lunch. I had thought most workers would be ensconced in their workplaces, parents had dropped off their little darlings at school and there would be relative calm. I was wrong. Traffic noise, of both the vehicular and human variety is incessant, with brake squeals, horn beeps and a constant hum of voices. Passing footsteps keep up a syncopated tattoo, which makes it hard to talk unless we shout. So much for a nice quiet brunch to catch up. Maybe it would have been better inside our favourite café.

I grab my serviette when a gust threatens to lift it from my lap. The only way to keep it down is to tuck it into the waistband of my slacks. Head down, I catch a whiff of the crispy bacon on the side of my dish. Yum. I gently stab the egg yolk and smile as it leaks then dribbles over the mashed avocado.

I nod to Ally. 'Hoe in while it's hot.' Her hashbrowns are nice and crispy brown. Wish I'd added a couple to my order. I stick the fork into the corner, slice, cut, lift and spot her eyes, which have widened. Her mouth drops open. One hand waves like a frantic flag caught in a storm.

'What's wrong?' I pop the morsel into my mouth, savour the rich yolk mixed with avocado.

Ally drops her cutlery, shoots up from her chair, gasps something incomprehensible and points. Her serviette flutters to the ground at the same time her cup rattles in the saucer and coffee splatters over the rim.

'Run,' she shouts, turns and heads for the café door. Her chair wobbles and falls.

Stunned, I jerk my head around. A black sedan careens and sways. Headed towards our table. Tyres squeal. The driver is hard to make out but not the terror on her face. Her arms on the steering wheel jolt. The car swings away. Then back.

Despite all the screams, my brain cells manage to sort themselves out and I scramble from my seat and curse when the toe of my sandal catches on a table leg. I tug. The leg screeches. The table totters and tips my plate to the ground. Too scared to care, I slam my body against the hard café wall just in time to see the car race past on two wheels. There is a thump when it drops onto its side. A screech of metal hurts the eardrums. Another almighty thump – the car wraps itself around the corner light post.

My held breath hurtles out as my legs buckle and I slither to the ground, still cold from the shade of the eaves. Feet slam past while my innards freeze into a solid mass. Spilt coffee is strong but doesn't drown out burnt rubber, exhaust and something acrid.

'Are you okay?' Ally crouches beside me.

Even though I'm not sure I nod.

'I need to help.'

Off course she does. She's a nurse. I nod again and wave her away.

Loud voices, groans and intermittent sobs fill my ears as I manage to get to my feet and stumble towards the chaos. Panicked people hover around, yank on mangled car doors, hold up mobile phones – so sick. A loud crack and they scatter. 'Watch out!' echoes from several with fingers pointe up. My eyes move in the same direction and I scuffle backwards as the wooden pole shivers, shakes, trembles and falls. Down, down, down – and crushes the side of the car.

What each voice utters is indistinguishable but in an instant a heavy silence hits with all eyes on the devastation. Red blood drip, drip, drips from the wreckage.

A Diner's Point of View
Alwena Willis

The sun shone with not a cloud in the sky and Sarah was eager to see Sue, now that her travels were over. Sarah chose a table outside and ordered cola for Sue and a chocolate milkshake for herself. She looked around. It was pleasant when the kids were back at school; everything seemed less hectic and definitely less noisy. She also loved this cafe where they met for brunch. She loved the tables outside under the yellow awning with flower boxes filled with shades of pink, yellow and lilac. Their scent wafted softly with the slight breeze. The tables were glass topped and the chairs very comfortable which is probably why she and Sue stayed here long after brunch. The traffic was not too bad, which would help with their conversation as when it was busy they often had to make their way inside. The light traffic meant they could sit outside on such a beautiful day. Jenny, one of the waitresses, brought out the drinks. As they were frequent visitors, they knew most of the staff by name. Placing the drinks on the table, the milkshake in front of her, and the coke opposite her, Jenny smiled.

'So, she's back then.'

'Yes, she's been home a few days so we will be back with our routine, well at least until that husband of hers drags her off on another adventure.' Sarah laughed.

'No way, I have told him I want a break and stay home for a change.' Sue leaned down and gave Sarah a hug and a smile at Jenny.

'I will leave the menu for you to ponder, come in when you are ready to order,' said Jenny.

'Thanks, Jenny,' they both said in unison, looked at each other and smiled.

'Well have you missed me?' asked Sue.

'Of course. I've had no one to listen to my baleful stories while you were away. It's not the same messaging you.'

'I know, I missed you for the same reason.'

With the cool breeze, Sarah was glad she wore a sleeveless top. The sun seemed extra bright so she slipped her sunglasses on, as did Sue. The glare was worse for Sue as she faced the sun. They slipped into their normal easy conversation when something caught her eye. She glanced up, tensed and held her breath. A black sedan was speeding and swerving towards them. She stood and watched in horror as it approached them, almost as if it was in slow motion. A woman was slumped over the driver's wheel. Horrified, Sarah witnessed the car come to a sudden stop, metal crashing, as it hit the lamppost just a few metres away.

'What an earth?' Sue said as Sarah slumped back into her seat.

A couple of metres more and it would have crashed into their table. Sue turned her attention to Sarah, as patrons and staff poured out the cafe. Sarah wanted to get up and help but her body seemed to be frozen. She heard Sue talking to her but it sounded like she was far away, and her eyes still focused on the black sedan.

A man from inside the cafe had opened the car door on the passenger side, leant over and turned the engine off. Petrol and exhaust fumes made their way to her lungs causing her to cough as her body attempted to remove the acrid air.

Sue got up, went around the table to grab Sarah by her shoulders and shake her gently.

'Sarah! Are you alright? Sarah!' Her voice full of anxiety as she looked at Sarah's pale face.

Dazed Sarah looked at her friend and frowned.

'Sarah, are you alright? You have had a shock, drink some of your shake.' She lifted the drink to Sarah's lips and encouraged her to take a few sips. For a moment Sarah thought she was going to vomit but managed to quell it. With tearful eyes she looked at Sue.

'I thought we were going to die, but the car seemed to swerve at the last minute and hit the post. Is the woman all right?'

Just then Jenny walked back from the accident. 'Police and ambulance are on the way, but the driver is already gone,' she said quietly. Are you two all right because you had a close escape?'

'We will be,' Sue answered, 'but I think we will shift ourselves to an inside table If you don't mind as Sarah has had a shock.'

'Of course, make your way in, I'll bring your drinks.'

Sue gathered her bag and gently pulled Sarah up, grabbing her bag as well. She guided the still shaking Sarah inside to a table well in and away from all the commotion outside. Jenny brought the drinks in and placed them on the table,

'Would you like me to bring a cup of sweet tea for Sarah?'

'Oh, that would be perfect, thank you.'

Sue sat next to Sarah, rubbing her cold hands. 'How are you feeling now.'

Sarah looked at Sue. 'Better thank you, it was just such a shock. I thought we were gone for sure. Poor lady, her poor family.'

Just then Jenny came with two cups of tea. 'They are on the house, drink it while it's hot, it's good for shock.'

Sarah and Sue mouthed, 'Thank you.'

Sarah turned her head and watched the police cars, fire trucks and ambulance pass by and park. She wished they didn't have to the sirens blaring. One by one the sirens ceased. She drank the sweet cup of tea, felt the colour return to her cheeks and her body warm up again. She wondered what happened to their lovely sunny day with the breeze blowing her hair lightly, and her eagerness to see Sue again. She glanced at Sue; aware she had been too wrapped up in her own feelings that she had not paid attention to Sue.

Sue smiled back. 'I'm fine, I heard it all but it must have been worse for you watching it.'

'Just when you wanted some peace and a relief from an adventure. I bet you didn't expect this today.'

'No not the pleasant morning I expected, but at least we are both safe. Someone is looking down on us.'

'Not like that poor woman,' Sarah said.

'No not her. But then I believe it was just her time to go. Let's get you home.' Placing her arm over Sarah, Sue guided her out of the cafe advising her not to look at the emergency services dealt with the wreckage of the crash. They had stared death in the face and escaped

A Server's Point of View
Dot Wilson

I let out a sigh as I grabbed the two plates of food from the counter and headed out to the alfresco area of the restaurant. It was a glorious day, warmer than usual, and the tables outside were all occupied, so I was too busy to appreciate the sunshine filtering through the Japanese cherry trees lining the footpath, or the heady scent of the pink blossoms which covered them. It didn't help that my boyfriend, Greg, had broken up with me the night before; he was heading overseas and didn't see any future in our relationship. Besides, he had to save for his trip.

So, here I am, eyes still puffy from crying myself to sleep, hastily applied makeup and hair caught in a messy ponytail, delivering two plates of seafood linguine to the loved-up couple at the table nearest the roadside. I mentally rolled my eyes as I approached, they were so nauseating, holding hands across the fake marble melamine tabletop and gazing into each other's eyes. As I got closer, I put on my best fake smile and placed the plates on the table, deriving a rather petty sense of satisfaction as they sat back and pulled their hands away to allow me to put their meals down.

Suddenly the peaceful atmosphere of the normally quiet suburban street was interrupted by the sound of a car approaching far too fast. I looked up to see a black sedan careering down the road towards the crossroads. I could just make out the woman at the wheel, looking terrified as the seemingly out of control vehicle mounted the kerb on the opposite side of the road and crashed into a lamp post, narrowly missing a teenage boy who was skateboarding along the footpath and a man who had just crossed.

The sound of the impact was deafening; I shook my head to try to rid my ears of the high-pitched ringing noise. For what seemed like an age but was only a second or two, the scene froze as people processed what had just happened.

Then chaos ensued as some ran to the aid of the driver, others dialled the emergency services on mobile phones. My two customers had gone to help the driver, so I ran back into the restaurant to tell Gino, my boss, what had just happened, but of course he had heard it and had come out to see what was going on. We nearly collided in the doorway.

I didn't know what to do. I hovered among the tables for a bit, feeling rather useless, then I crossed the road to see if I could be of any assistance. As I reached the kerb, a dark blue Audi cruised slowly past. The male driver looked intently at the scene. There was something slightly sinister about his cold stare and lack of expression. Suddenly the car accelerated and disappeared around the next corner.

I had never seen a car crash up close before; the twisted metal wrapped around the lamp post was both horrific and fascinating. There was a smell of burning plastic although, thank goodness, there were no visible flames. They had managed to get the gent who had been almost hit, from out of the ditch where he ended up in his haste to escape. A middle-aged lady, who seemed to know what she was doing, was tending to him, giving him mouth-to-mouth. I felt pretty superfluous and made a mental note to enrol in a first aid course in the near future.

'Can I do anything to help?' I asked.

'I think we've got things under control here, thanks. The ambulance should be here soon.' she turned her attention back to the man, who had a weird grin on his face.

The driver was still in the car, with a man crouched down on the road beside her. She seemed to be unconscious. In the distance I could hear the sound of sirens as the emergency vehicles approached. Since there was nothing I could do to be of any help, I turned to head back to the restaurant. Something lying in the gutter caught my eye. It was a flash drive. The man's shoulder bag lay nearby, its contents spilled out across the footpath. I picked everything up and put them back into the bag. His wallet, mobile phone, keys. All safely returned. I put the bag down beside the woman who was rendering assistance to him.

'Here's his bag. Everything had fallen out, but I've collected it all and put it back.'

'Oh great, thanks. I'll make sure it goes in the ambulance with him.'

My fingers curled around the flash-drive, and I thrust my hand deep into my pocket. I don't know why I did it. It's not like they're expensive or anything. I needed a new one, my old one was full, and this was a pretty fancy looking model, quite futuristic in fact. I figured he wouldn't miss it or would think it was lost in the wreck.

Had I known what repercussions that small, petty, stupid act were about to bring down on me, I would have crawled back on my hands and knees and handed the damned thing over and begged his forgiveness.

The Driver's Point of View
Nicole Corsini

The Jim Beam stubby in one hand and mobile phone in the other, didn't leave me with many usable fingers to hold the cars keys. Under normal circumstances, I would have thought to put the phone in my pocket or put the stubby down. Better yet under normal circumstances, I would have been sober and wouldn't have had the stubby at all.

The keys fell onto the sand where the grass had struggled to grow through the relentless summer heat. It was harder to pick them up than anticipated. I hovered somewhere in between bent right over and standing upright. Jim Beam spilled from the bottle, splashed onto the ground, sending bourbon mud up the bottom of my jeans. Any further movement towards the floor I was going to end up down there myself.

I stared at the keys, willing them to jump up into my hands, the stupidness of the situation made me laugh. The brain wasn't working with the body or was it that the body wouldn't listen to the brain. It was now or never; I took the chance and bent all the way down with the phone still held awkwardly between the thumb and index finger and managed to scoop up the keys with the three fingers.

With a triumphant smirk I straighten myself quickly - too quick. Unsteady on my feet, I stumbled sideways onto the car door. The keys slid against the metallic black paint of my 2013 Mazda 3 and left a decent scratch down the panel. 'Shit!' I said, mad about the paint but also impressed I managed to not spill the drink again.

It took a minute to collect myself before I pushed my dead body weight upright. I fumbled through the keys and pressed the right button to unlock all the doors. The stubby gripped tight, I used the index finger to lift the handle, pull the door towards me and poured what was left in the bottle down my arm.

Once I managed to get into the driver's seat, I chucked the empty bottle onto the passenger seat floor. Then folded down the visor and examined the reflection in the mirror, surprised at how terrible it looked. I needed to get home and sleep.

Belt plugged in, key in the ignition, engine started, checked and rearranged mirrors – time to drive. See, you're fine to drive, I encouraged myself. Being overly cautious, I slowly backed out of the driveway onto the road. The sun, halfway up the sky, shined bright into the car and exaggerated the dirty state of the windows.

I shouldn't have been driving. All that self-encouragement had been to silence the deeper voice that told me how stupidly dangerous it was. Food had always helped to sober me up, so I decided to detour through the main shopping strip near my house and get some take-away.

There was a lot more life out than I was expecting, the sudden busyness made me anxious. In an attempt to drown out the world around me, I turned up the radio until it was the only thing I could hear.

Shops and cafes lined both sides of the street the whole way down with speed bumps every two hundred metres to slow the traffic for regular pedestrians crossing. The café outdoor sitting areas were filled with people enjoying breakfast before the day would become too hot to be outside.

The repetitive slow down, up the bump, down the bump, speed up motion made me feel nauseous, while the sun that glared into my face forced the headache I was expecting to have later that day to come early. I needed to get home right away.

At the upcoming intersection the traffic lights were green. 'Stay green, stay green, stay green!' I pleaded. As if wanting to do exactly the opposite of what I asked, the orange light appeared. I could make it. My foot fell heavy on the accelerator. The engine revved loudly and the car took off. Heads from both sides of the street turned towards the sudden noise and shook in disapproval. I didn't care, I just needed to get home.

The light turned red; I wasn't going to make it but I also wasn't going to stop. There was no time to think, I pressed my foot to the floor. Too fast. It happened in a second and in slow motion at the same time. The screams were louder than the music, I couldn't tell if it was coming from me or outside of the car. There was a flash of a person in front of me, there and gone. Then nothing. Stillness, silence and darkness.

It was sound that returned to me first. The loud music was gone and yelling voices took its place. There was banging on the window, each knock pounded in my head. Pain was next, it appeared in every part of my body like nothing I had felt before. I tried to make sense of what was happening around me, tried to open my eyes and lift my head off of the steering wheel but the brain and body still weren't cooperating. I was pulled back into darkness.

Another knock on the window woke me. 'Hello! An ambulance is on its way, they will get you out. I need you to wake up for me alright?' a muffled voice came through the glass.

The doors, unable to be opened, had been damaged along with the whole front of the car. Wrapped around the metal light post that now bent slightly.

My legs were trapped beneath the crumpled dash, I wouldn't have been able to move even if I could try so I stayed in stillness.

Blood ran heavy from my nose but the scent of deployed airbag still passed through. Ambulance sirens crept up from the distance as the muffled voice spoke again, Stay awake, the ambulance is almost here!' followed by three more knocks on the window. It hurt too much; I wanted silence.

I didn't want to stay awake. I wanted to go back to where the pain went away. A cry escaped my body, taking with it the air that was in my lungs. The air drawn back in was replaced with blood. It was all too much. I couldn't do it anymore. I had to go back to nothingness.

Lamp Post's Point of View
Tania Park

The noise sets my molecules thrumming, sending uncomfortable messages along every cellulose fibre. A loud, long squeal is followed in an instant by an acrid stench of rubber searing across bitumen. Everything inside me tightens as human screams split the air, louder but not drowning out the still screeching high-pitched squeal.

Below me, humans at tables in the various eateries lining the busy road, scatter in all directions, leaving behind upturned China, dribbles of aromatic spilt liquids, half-eaten plates of food and bright coloured paper napkins floating, hovering in the draft of wind before falling in graceful arcs to the brick pavement.

Whump!

The sudden pain is intense as metal tears apart to wrap itself around me, the raw edges biting and grinding into my old, outer grey layer; hugging so tight it's as though life is being squeezed out of me. My molecules jam together in places they shouldn't fit but they fight to gain equilibrium and find their normal place. Despite this, my inner fibres splinter apart, the same agony as when the smoke-drenched chainsaw hacked through me and dropped me to the ground twenty-five years ago. The agony that day was unbearable as thread sheared from thread, cell from cell. Like a slow domino effect, fibre after fibre parted company, tearing apart my innards until I thundered to the ground with an echoing thud of agony.

Now, a fizz of electricity, which runs through the orange plastic pipe stapled all the way up my spine, hisses, heats and spits before splitting the atmosphere with a loud sharp crack and blinding flash, leaving behind the stench of black billowing smoke, which rises up, up, up to dissipate.

At my foot, amongst the mangled debris of plastic, rubber and metal, intermittent groans mingle with painful sobs as fleshy bits stretch and quiver. Fingers tremble: an arm wavers in the air before it flops on an agonising groan. Wisps of metallic scents hover and rise from the red liquid pooling in the wreckage before it drip, drip, drips down my side: *plip, plip, plip*. Still the red holds warmth but it quickly cools in the night air.

As the colour of the world around me begins to fade and turn grey, my uppermost two thirds begin to wobble and I know. This maniacal human who had so often thought the road before me was her personal racetrack, has robbed me of the life I know as a guiding light in the darkness. With the last of my strength, I concentrate hard on forcing every atom to flow in one direction as my fibres continue to shred. Joy fills my soul as I crash down, down, down to crush the metal into groaning human until I hear the last gasp of her life. Justice!

Love Me Tinder
Garry Davies

A short story of a modern romance, set in 1882

Lucy, who in her time had made more than one heart burn, drew her hooded cloak tightly against herself and crossed the narrow, gas-lit street towards the man with the matches. 'Are you Earnest?' she asked.

'No, I'm Arthur. Which one are you?'

'I'm Verity,' said Lucy.

'Aah, Miss Forthright, we were expecting you. Please come with me.' Arthur led her into a large room. She could see that it was mostly filled with small tables. Each table had two chairs. A candle provided a dim light for each setting. More than half of the tables were occupied by either one or two people. So that he could look at her, he led her to a well-lit corner where she loosened her cloak and pulled back her hood and let it fall upon her shoulders. Arthur openly took in the full effect of her curly auburn hair which, she knew, showed to good effect against the dark green of the cloak. 'Yes, yes, that will do very nicely. Very nicely indeed. Very diverting. I don't think you should have any trouble at all in setting the target alight.'

He indicated a table across the room. Lucy pulled her cloak tight and led the way to where they sat down. Arthur took a small, tightly filled packet from his inner-breast pocket and slid it across the table. She glanced at it but did not pick it up. She could see a name on it: Verity Forthright. 'These are the matches you will use. Wait until I am gone and until the first man approaches. If he is not suitable, use the matches. Someone will be watching.'

Arthur left through the same door they entered moments before. She waited. Then a shadow fell across the table. She looked up. A tall man stood before her. 'Verity?' he asked.

'Yes.'

He placed a similar unopened packet on the table. He raised an eyebrow. 'My credentials.' Lucy looked at the packet. Earnest Swiperight was written across it in the same hand as that on her own package. 'You are very pretty.'.

'Thank you,' said Lucy. She stood. 'I'm Verity Forthright. I'm pleased to meet you.' She offered her hand which he briefly took, smiled and indicated that she should sit. He laid his hat on the table and unbuttoned his heavy coat. He took his time, being careful with the way he went about the task, and then he sat.

Lucy took the opportunity to glance at her prospect. First impressions were important, she knew. There could be no mistakes, often one chance was all there was. She would have to act on instinct and, perhaps live with her decision for ever.

'It's a risk, isn't it,' he smiled at her, reading her mind.

Lucy looked for hidden meaning in his face. A trap. He knows what I'm thinking, she worried.

'What?' is all she could manage to say.

'This is. A risk, what we are doing now.'

'Oh! Yes, I suppose it is. But still, there's always a way out, isn't there. I mean, we both have our matches.'

'I hope we don't use them,' he said kindly to her. 'But, yes, if we must, then we can use them.' He paused and then continued. 'Tell me about yourself, Verity. How do you come to be here, what are you looking for?'

'Perhaps if you start …' she trailed off into silence.

'Yes, of course. Well my name is Earnest Swiperight, as you know …'

Is it, she thought? Is this whole thing going to be a lie? She glanced at the fake name on her own packet.

'… and I have a small business where I live. A print shop where I publish the shire weekly paper …'

Yes, yes, I know, her thoughts raced away again. That's why I'm here, your business, your paper. You.

'… and there has been some trouble and so I thought I should meet someone. Someone who could — well you know, help me with …,' this time Earnest faltered.

He seemed so open up to this point but it was as though he couldn't bring himself to finally speak. Perhaps he wasn't sure. That must be it, he wasn't sure. They had only just met and any sort of commitment would be absurd at this time.

'Well, you do seem to be …,' Lucy searched for words.

'Earnest,' he offered. 'It's important.'

She smiled for the first time in his company. She relaxed her grip on the cloak and looked directly into the face of the honest printer who had trouble with publishing his weekly newspaper.

'My name's not Verity,' she began. 'Neither is it Forthright.'

'Well, in that case, no it's not. Not very forthright at all.' He smiled.

'It's Lucy. Lucy Asher. I was nervous, unsure. Lots of the girls do it. For protection.'

'Do you need to be protected, Lucy? You seem to be more than capable to me.'

'Tell me about the trouble at the paper,' she changed the subject.

He looked at her, still not sure if he was put off by the deception. He paused for a brief moment, then made up his mind and continued, 'There's someone who is dishonestly using public money, a developer, and I have nearly been able to prove his guilt. I only need one more piece of evidence before I can take it to the authorities. But I am working on my own and I need a — well someone to share the burden of running my print shop. My home. You understand?'

'I do,' said Lucy. She could be decisive. She had made up her mind. 'Take up your matches, Earnest, we are leaving. Together,' she added. Earnest stood and hastily put on his hat and roughly buttoned his coat. He took his named package to the open fire, threw it in, and strode to the door, hoping he had found his flame.

Lucy followed. She slipped her packet into her pocket but pretended to throw it in to the fire. This relationship was, after all, started with a lie. She would take the job. She would take Earnest. But when the evidence was collected, the developer would pay her well to use the matches on it.

RED
Victoria Mizen

Passion, fire, love and hate
she's totally consuming,
demands our full attention.

Birds see red and head for food
in Eucalypts, Callistemons,
Grevilleas and more.

Man brings roses, long and red
to woo his mate,
adding hearts painted red
on cards that say
'I love you.'

But when love dies
and hearts turn cold,
when faces red with anger,
reveal the pain, the loss they bear,
then love can turn to hate.

In the hearth the fire glows
with flames that give red heat
to warm the home
and comfort lonely hearts

On summer days when temperatures
are way above the norm,
the sight, the smell and sound of flames
flash warnings –
This red is hell.

Weather, Weirdos and Whingeing
Su Watson

Su lay in the van and stared up at the fuzzy ceiling in the dark. Outside, the *whoomph whoomph*, of the awning, as it did battle with the 40kmph gusts, did nothing to ease her into oblivion. She unclenched her jaw and tried to stop twitching at every sound. Feeling the heavy breathing of the van, all around her, as its vinyl walls bellowed in and out, only reinforced her impression it was in a fight for its life. How could anyone sleep in this? Beside her, Van-man did some heavy breathing of his own.

'Nothing to worry about,' he'd grumbled when she'd dug him in the ribs an hour ago. 'The pegs are securely in the concrete, and that huge green van next to us will shelter the van from the brunt.' And with that, he'd rolled over and continued his snuffling sounds as though she hadn't woken him.

Her mind wandered to the huge green van. When they'd pulled into the park, earlier in the afternoon, they'd initially been glad the attendant had thoughtfully placed them directly behind their oversized green neighbour.

'Shelter against the impending sea breeze,' she'd said.
Then, not two minutes after they'd finished setting up, and Van-man had knocked the last guy-rope peg into the concrete, with his 30lb lump hammer, the occupant of the large green van wandered around to greet them.

'Maaan, yooearrdostay?' But before they could answer, he continued, 'S'coool maaan. I mean, I cayezaday. Lassnyzablass maaan. Soooo many people.' And with that, he wandered away.

'What did he say?' Su whispered, as she and Van-man looked at each other.

Van-man shrugged. 'I think he arrived yesterday.'

She turned to put the kettle on, worrying about her hearing loss. She knew that crowded noisy rooms were already a problem for her, but now with no background noise she'd barely made out a word their neighbour had said. Behind her, Van-man was talking again but it wasn't to her.

'So close, maaan, ya sooo close!' Their neighbour seemed agitated.

'Nice truck,' Van-man offered to distract him 'Unusual.'

'Yeah maan, I co…'

Su switched off, rather than strain her brain trying to follow the indecipherable conversation. She scanned the tiny patch of sun-baked dirt that passed for a van park and stopped when she came to their neighbour's van. It was a truck, really. It looked like an old prime mover with a caravan welded onto the back. The whole thing towered above their own car and van combined and had a sturdy military quality to it, though Su reflected that the colour might enhance this. She nodded, and smiling politely, pretended to follow what was being said, while she turned away to tend to Kallie, the dog, who'd been asleep in the car.

'Faaar out, maaan. Sooo cuude. He traaaloo?'

Su turned at the unexpected silence and realised, as their neighbour looked from the dog to her, that he was expecting a response. Her brain whirred frantically.

'Yeah, she travels with us sometimes.'

Thank god! Van man to the rescue.

'She's pretty good, is happy to be outdoors and doesn't mind the long stretches in the car,' Van-man continued. 'The dog's a good traveller too.' His feeble joke sailed over the truck.

Kallie wagged her tail and trotted obligingly toward their squatting neighbour. He grabbed her and rubbed her roughly, squeezing her lower back as he went. She whimpered when he hit the arthritis in her hips and, wriggling away from him, headed back to the safety of the car.

'Mmm goowidoz,' he mumbled. Then, in a surprising turn of clarity, added, 'Ya beda av iz heart worm upta date. Lossa mozzies ere lass nigh. Coont geda a winka sleep all nigh.

Barstuds kept me awake till smornin. Theyull dofrim.' And with a glance in Kallie's direction, he was gone again.

Great, something else to worry about. They'd been on the road for 5 weeks and though she'd given Kallie her monthly heart-worm medication before they left, she knew it was now overdue. It was the one thing she'd forgotten to bring with her.

Reading Su's mind, Van-man patted her on the shoulder. 'I read somewhere heartworm medication is administered too often. There's a suspicion it lasts much longer than a month. Besides, with the wind getting up tonight, the mozzies won't be able to fly. Don't worry, come and have some tea.'

As they sat down to relax with their well-earned cuppa, a sudden blast of noise emanated from the green van and loud techno music began to pulse through the walls. The high-pitched, metallic sounds and incessant, fast frequency of the drum set Su's teeth on edge, and she felt anxious as her heart raced in time with the beat. Three minutes later, their neighbour reappeared, weaving towards Van-man's chair.

'Faaar out, man, ya so close, so close. Why ya so close? Space maaan.' He waved his arm toward the other empty spots in the campsite. 'Why ya par rye beyine me? So close?'

'Because the camp attendant put us here,' Van-man answered calmly. 'Maybe she knows more people will rock up before dark, you know—has bookings.'

'She tole ya? She tole ya to par here, rye ere beyine me? Farcking Nazi. Why she tell ya tha? Nazi! So much space, maan.' he was agitated again. 'Maybe ya cu mooove maaan.' Then, eyeing the pegs in the rock-hard ground, said 'Mebbe Arl moove.' He staggered round the side of the truck but was back a few seconds later. 'Ya lye my music though, ay maan? Snot too loud.' He was carrying a beautiful didgeridoo and attempted several aborted efforts to blow into it. He held it out toward Van-man. 'Ya wanna touch it?'

Van-man politely reached out and stroked the beautiful instrument. 'Well, now you mention it. Perhaps the music is a little loud.' Then, not wanting to seem overly complaining,

Van-man added, 'We like some of the stuff you were playing quietly when we arrived, but the loud techno stuff—not so much.'

'Oh no man, you're not Christian, are you? You are. You're Christian aren you?' He shook his head as if trying to clear a fog. 'Never mind, maan, s'OK, you'll lye my music... guarantee. When you ge used to it, maaan. I had a boss on the farm, who say get that farcking crap off, when I leff he's putting on raves maaan. Guarantee!' With that, he returned to his van and turned the music up.

Su went into their own van. A giggle erupted as she held her head in her hands. She wondered if hysteria was setting in. She thought of the cover of the brochure she'd seen Van-man furtively looking at three months ago. There was a fabulous turquoise sea bounded by gold and silver sand, as far as the eye could see. When she'd asked him, he'd said he was planning a romantic trip for Valentine's Day. She was surprised. Not normally given to romantic gestures, she thought she'd misheard him. But no, he told her to pack for the beach, and so she had dreamed of sun loungers and cocktail umbrellas right up until he had begun preparing the van.

Now she was lying in a mobile ensuite, experiencing a mini hurricane, and in the past five weeks, she hadn't seen so much as a swimsuit, never mind a cocktail umbrella. There'd been several incidents involving the gear box, necessitating trips to the mechanic. An extreme heatwave, an infection requiring antibiotics, gale force winds, an upset stomach, a fall on an uneven concrete pavement, and now an apparent dope fiend.

Van-man snored on, oblivious. He was having a great time. He wasn't at work. He was outdoors. He was exploring.

The van rocked violently in the wind. Su closed her eyes and practised calm thoughts. They would either still be here in the morning, or they would wake up and they wouldn't be in Kansas anymore. They would have to find their way home with an open topped van, and since they were currently remote, it would probably be without the help of the Wizard of Aus.

But then again, that was a worry for tomorrow. And looking at it from a different perspective—with an open top, it could be a long while before they would be ready for another trip! In the meantime, she'd dig out a few sun-drenched brochures of her own and leave them strategically around the house. She might even make a booking. After all, a couple of weeks in Italy, sipping cocktails from a sun-lounger, would surely be more cost-effective than the therapy she would need to endure another camping trip.

Christmas
Theo Pabst

Torn paper, string ad ribbons cut,
cries of joy from the children's lot.
Each one inspects and thinks about
their gift to be the best they got
then with their pressies, venture out.

Oldies looking on with envy
wishing they could swap with them.
For they could remember their bevy
when they were young and lissom.
Now, memories are just like a movie.

The turkey is on the table
ready to carve, all hoping for a leg,
but after a lot of babble,
there is nothing left to beg
stomachs full, just like in the fable.

It is over. There are stories to be told
and a new year to test us
with those resolutions to uphold.
But is it worth the fuss?
For will we be brave and hold.

Time to shop and fill the larder
For Christmas left us bare.
I must cut back, but that is harder
for I was never one to share.
Are they hot-cross-buns, I, see?